"Annie, listen," Jack said. "You made one mistake. Give yourself a break."

"You don't understand." She pulled away.

"Understand what?"

"That I'm falling in love with you!" Tears sprang to her eyes, and she covered her mouth with her hand.

The words drifted away; her eyes looked anywhere but at him. Annie wasn't going to say again that she was falling in love with him. In fact, Jack was certain she'd pay dearly to retrieve those words. But once spoken, the word "love" hung in the air like perfume.

"He hurt you a lot," he said.

"I was such a fool. I'd never been close to falling in love and getting married before I met Peter. I expected falling in love would be like settling onto a down comforter. But it was more like falling out of an airplane. First my main parachute failed. Then my reserve chute failed."

"So feeling attracted to me increases your fear."

She searched his face for any sign of disbelief, but instead she saw kindness. Concern. Sincerity. She swallowed hard and nodded.

"Do you want me to take you home? You call the shots."

Do I want...? Do I? Pros and cons battled in Annie's head. The job of umpire wore her out, but Jack was right. She had to call the shots.

He said he wouldn't rush me. She took a deep breath, exhaled slowly, and met his cool, unwavering gaze with one of her own.

And then...Jack Cabrini smiled. And Annie Riker could swear she heard the sound of her hard shell cracking. She had to wet her lips to say anything at all.

"I want to stay."

Bed, Bath & Beloved

by

Lynnette Baughman

BED, BATH & BELOVED

Cover Art by *Rae Monet*

The Wild Rose Press
PO Box 708
Adams Basin, NY 14410-0706
Visit us at www.thewildrosepress.com

Publishing History
First CHAMPAGNE Rose Edition, 2009
ISBN: 1-60154-762-5

Published in the United States of America

Dedication

To Bill.
Cherish is the word...

Available Now from The Wild Rose Press

Love with a Welcome Stranger
by Lynnette Baughman

Mandy McCay's life as a Hollywood starlet ended with a bullet from a deranged fan. Miraculously, she recovers, but there are gaps in her memory. Important gaps. The years her face and figure were splashed across tabloid pages are easy. But what happened the summer before she left Montana?

Like everyone in Mandy's hometown, Campbell West followed her medical miracle on TV. He's not prepared for her to come home more beautiful than ever, or for the sudden new attraction between them. At least, Mandy thinks it's new. Cam—God help him!—remembers every inch of her body! When should he tell her of their passionate love, her betrayal, and his pain? Or can he risk forgetting it all—and hoping she'll never remember?

Lovin' Montana
by Lynnette Baughman

Rand Monahan arrives in Montana with a bad attitude. After a heart attack and three months of cardiac rehab, the Wall Street millionaire is on a "relax or die" vacation.

Luanne Holt knows she needs to look forward, but she's mired in the past. After her fiancé died, she took up the legal battle to get his valuable solar cell patent back from the Wall Street scoundrels who took it. She won't let herself love again until the solar cell factory is open in Bitter Falls.

But Rand Monahan and the tidal pull of the autumn moon are tugging her heart toward the future.

Chapter One

Annie Riker slid her oversized sunglasses to the top of her head and collapsed like a folding stroller into an Adirondack chair.

In the chair beside her on the unmowed front lawn of Albion House, her sister Tess opened one eye. Closed it.

"Welcome back."

"Glad to be home." Annie watched a doe peer out of a laurel hedge and step cautiously to a patch of fresh grass. Right behind her crept twin fawns. Moments like this reminded Annie why she loved living in small-town Montana. Maybe when she'd lived here for five or ten years she wouldn't even glance at the deer, but she didn't think that could happen.

The doe looked at her—stared at her—and Annie could swear they communicated, mother to mother.

You know what it's like, said the mom of two Bambis. *You know how dangerous the world is, how hard it is to keep a child safe.*

"How was Missoula?" Tess asked.

"Good. I brought some fabric samples for the loveseats and the drapes. And—here's the best news—I bought two antique library tables and three armoires." She picked up the insulated carafe on the low table between the chairs. "Is this decaf?"

"Yes, but I don't know if it's still hot."

Annie poured a cup of coffee and tasted it. "It's...okay. You want some?"

"No, thanks. I'm too tired to swallow." Both eyes closed.

Annie had parked in back, so she knew there were at least two dozen men working inside and behind the house. Out here, however, it was peaceful. The wild jungle of lilacs that had taken over the east side of the mansion perfumed the air.

It had been a hot day, unusual for mid-May in northwest Montana. She'd heard people say they'd seen snow on June first in Bitter Falls. Sure, they'd said snow that late in the spring was a rare event, but—still. Snow?

Or were the farmers and truckers at the Roundup Café pulling her leg? She and Tess had a long way to go before they'd be considered "locals."

Officially, their roots in Bitter Falls went back one full century, but they'd known about their great-great-grandmother and their inheritance for only a year and three months.

A clutch of her stomach reminded her how desperately she wanted to belong in this small, all-American town, how she wanted this to be home for herself and her daughter. Savannah, five-and-a-half, was crazy about Montana; she had been since the day they'd driven across the state line.

Tess moaned and rubbed the back of her neck. "I'm in pain. I need a massage."

Annie resisted the urge to say, *I told you so.* Instead she said, "You've made a lot of progress, haven't you?"

Tess began scraping paint off the old porch railings early that morning, before Annie and Savannah left.

"Progress?" Tess rotated her right wrist and rubbed it with her left hand. "About twelve feet is all. And yes, you were correct. The entire railing is going back on the list of jobs we pay for. It's not like we can't afford it."

Soft buzzing drew Annie's gaze to the wildflowers around them. Bees were equal-opportunity pollinators, visiting the lowliest clover and fireweed with the same manners as they would a Princess Diana rose. When she and Tess got serious about having a lawn, the riff-raff would have to go, but right now she was on the side of the bees.

She snapped the stem of a wild daisy and couldn't resist plucking the petals, saying "loves me, loves me not" to herself. It ended with "loves me."

Oh yeah? Then who is he? And when will he show up in my life?

She tossed the stem away and frowned. Even daisies are wrong fifty percent of the time.

At least they don't tell deliberate lies. In that way, daisies are better than men.

Instead of facing south, to the panoramic view of distant mountains that their bed and breakfast guests would admire, Annie and Tess faced Albion House.

"Staring up at the house is like watching the opening of a horror movie." Annie laughed. "With a full moon and the wrong music, this place would scare the pants off me."

"And yet you've never been happier," Tess observed as she threaded her fingers through her shoulder-length brown hair and swept it away from her face.

Annie had tired of her own long hair and gotten a short 'do. The young woman at the only beauty shop in Bitter Falls called it a pixie, but Annie said a woman her height, five feet ten inches, couldn't pass for a pixie anywhere. Whatever the name, she liked the wash-and-wear freedom of the style. A little dab of gel and a run-through of her fingers was all it needed.

"Savannah loves it here," Tess added.

"That she does," Annie agreed. "We had a good time shopping in Missoula. I had to drag her away from the pet store, of course, and she was in a foul mood for about fifteen minutes, but I convinced her it's better to wait to get a puppy."

"You convinced her? Tell me another fairy tale."

Annie sighed. "I told her that we need to choose a dog that was born in Bitter Falls so it can visit its family."

Tess laughed. "And she bought that?"

"Yes, and I expect you to agree with my wise counsel."

"Don't I always?" Tess sat forward and poured herself half a cup of the old coffee. She tasted it and made a face. "This stuff is awful."

"You're pickier than I am," Annie said with a lofty tone.

"You say that like it's a bad thing," Tess said. "Besides, I'm not picky. I have discriminating taste."

Annie watched Savannah run from the east end of the mansion, location of the only operational bathroom at this stage of the project, wearing her sunflower swimsuit and flip-flops. The deer family bounded for the protection of the laurel.

"Mommy, can I turn on the sprinkler?"

"May I?" Annie corrected automatically. "Yes. Just don't spray us."

"Don't be too hasty," Tess said. "It might feel good. I thought it didn't get hot here until July."

"The weather pattern is unpredictable, or so they say. If today is any indication, it might be a long, hot summer."

"There are forest fires in Washington already," Tess said with a sigh. "Dry lightning."

"Yeah. I hate that." Annie watched Savannah sprint back and forth through the sprinkler.

"We used to do that," Tess said.

"Yeah," Annie said softly, "I remember. I wish Mom could see her. It's sad that she won't have any memory of Mom at all."

Annie was grateful, at least, that Diana had held her granddaughter. Already in hospice care for her unrelenting cancer, she'd told them that she'd be watching Savannah from heaven.

Tears seeped from the corners of Annie's eyes, and she sopped them up with her knuckles.

"I wonder what Mom would say if she could see Albion House," Tess mused. "An inheritance from a great-grandmother she never heard of."

Annie stared at the mansion they'd nicknamed the Money Pit and groaned. "She would probably say we're out of our minds to believe it will be ready for guests by Labor Day."

When they'd received the letter from the estate attorney, fifteen months ago, saying the two of them were the long-lost heirs to a fortune, they'd been more stunned than if they'd won the lottery. Because to win the lottery, they'd have to consciously buy a ticket. For this they did nothing. Had no clue that their mom's birth father was the only grandchild of a fabulously wealthy and bitterly lonely pioneer of the Klondike Gold Rush.

How had the San Francisco law firm of Dusart and Dusart tracked them down? They still didn't have the whole story, but a box of correspondence between Goldie Jones and the firm, plus the chronological report of the detective agency the law firm had retained five years ago, was due to arrive within a few days.

From the moment Annie and Tess stepped through the door of Albion House, they were smitten. No, more than that. They were in love. But getting builders to even look at the project, much less bid seriously on doing the job, had been an exercise in pain and insults. Two contractors had gone so far as to recommend tearing the "eyesore" down and starting over.

It wasn't for lack of money to pay for the work. Goldie Jones had left them a fortune in the First National Bank along with fifty acres and Albion House, the Great-White-Elephant on top of Albion Hill.

Discouraged, the two of them had talked it over.

The only way they would go ahead with gutting and reconstructing the old place, then remodeling the interior to suit their business model, was if they had an ironclad contract with a top-notch general contractor.

Great Western had shown interest, but interest wasn't going to be enough, especially considering that it was a huge company. With headquarters in Denver, Great Western had projects all over seven western states. Albion House could get lost in the shuffle.

It had been Duke Hemmer's love for the old mansion that sealed the deal. He shared their vision, blurry though it was, of wanting to restore Albion House's beauty and essential character while reconstructing its insides to twenty-first century standards. Form plus function.

When Duke and his team started the work on Albion House, his competence and confidence made Annie think of John Wayne, riding to the rescue at the head of the cavalry.

He was old enough to be her father, and not the least bit attractive, but she was a tiny bit in love with him. In a comforting, favorite-uncle way.

Duke Hemmer had earned her trust, and trust was a hard, hard sell with Annie Riker. She'd made one huge mistake, trusting the wrong man, and that meteorite had burned up in spectacular fashion when it fell out of the sky.

True, the two "trust" scenarios had nothing in common. Relying on Duke and Great Western Construction was a business relationship. Strictly business.

Not the sticky, squishy, sweaty kind of relationship. The relationship she'd had with Peter. The kind of relationship that cuts a woman's heart out. How did the country western song put it?

She grinned. Oh, yeah. *You Done Tore Out My Heart And Stomped That Sucker Flat.*

The grin evaporated. When it came to Peter, humor was long gone.

A door closing behind them caught Annie's attention. She turned and slid her sunglasses down to cut the glare of the late afternoon sun. Down at the street, beyond the enormous lawn, a tall man walked around the front of a big Ford pickup.

The workmen always drove up the road to the far side of Albion Hill and parked in back of the mansion. And none of them drove a truck like that one. Candy-apple red and shiny as a sports car in a showroom.

Furthermore, the man standing on the sidewalk didn't look like a construction guy.

Well, he had the build for it. Broad shoulders, muscles. But not the clothes. She watched him reach into the cab behind the front seat, pull out a sports coat, and put it on. His pale blue shirt was open at the neck.

"That truck is sexy as sin," Annie murmured.

Tess leaned around the wide chair to get a look and then stood. "You're looking at the truck? Girl, you need an eye exam. Or therapy."

"I've had therapy. It didn't work."

"Try again. Not all men are like you-know-who."

Annie stood to watch the stranger climb the limestone stairs, in three sections, cut into the steep hillside. He took his time, stopping to survey the view at each stone landing.

Her opinion was that he got better looking the closer he came to them. He wore dark aviator glasses, and she itched to see his eyes.

Okay, she admitted to herself. I'm itching to see a lot more than his eyes. There's something about the way he moves that makes my mouth dry. Graceful, like an athlete. Confident. Dark hair, thick. Nice tan.

Against her will, her tongue traced her lips; she hoped he didn't see it. Or maybe she hoped he did. It had been a long, long time since she'd noticed a man the way she noticed this fine specimen.

Not since Peter Dylan. A.k.a. Joseph Dylan, Sheldon Dylan, and Sheldon Roth. Also known—to her—as Lying Sack of Shit.

She tried to summon up anger. Anger was a good solid emotion she could grab and hang onto. Anger was good. Protective, like a suit of armor and a shield and lance.

But all she could feel was shame. Nobody had forced her to believe Peter's lies. She'd leapt off that cliff all by herself.

The anger she'd hoarded for six years was washed out now. Diluted. Like one lemon squeezed into ten gallons of water. Because however stupid she'd been to fall for Peter, however amoral and self-centered he was, the result of that dangerous liaison was one perfect miracle. *Savannah.*

For the millionth time, she thanked God that Savannah looked like her, and like Tess and their mom, instead of Peter. Well, except for her eyes. Those were Peter's. Blue-green. Shimmering like water flowing through a coral reef, instead of common everyday blue, like hers.

The stranger in the sports coat took off his glasses, folded the sides, and slid them into a pocket inside his jacket. His eyes were cinnamon brown with flecks of copper. Warm, observant, direct. Confident.

"Hello. I'm Jack Cabrini."

Annie knew the name, of course; she'd seen his signature on their lengthy construction contract. The CEO of Great Western Construction.

Tess thrust out her hand and welcomed him. Annie did the same.

"Ann-Marie Riker. Call me Annie." She kept her eyes on his face, but she wanted to walk around him like she would a hologram. See him from all angles. *Damn!*

"Duke isn't here," Tess said. "I haven't seen him since yesterday morning."

"I know," he said. "I've made some major changes in the company. I needed Duke to take over a commercial project in Wyoming. He was the only one with the engineering background I could tap on short notice."

"Duke's—what? Duke's gone?" A break in Annie's voice revealed her shock.

Cold washed over her like a sudden blizzard out of Alberta.

They'd signed the contract with Great Western, and—yes—the name on the bottom line was Jackson T. Cabrini. But it was Duke Hemmer they'd counted on, relied on, believed in to see the project through to completion.

The formal contract had involved more negotiation than getting troops out of a war zone. But the more important contract was the handshake with Duke.

And now this stranger strolls up our hill and says that Duke is gone.

Her first thought when Jack Cabrini took off his sunglasses was that he belonged on a calendar, wearing a loincloth.

Now she pictured him as Mister January on the CEO Calendar. Rich, handsome, in a custom tuxedo, with ice water in his veins. How could she have thought his eyes were warm?

Tess cleared her throat. "Duke can't be gone."

"Yes. I'm afraid so," Cabrini said. "He's already on the job in Wyoming."

"He didn't tell us!" Annie was awash with anger and disbelief, as if she'd surfaced from a scuba dive and discovered that her dive boat had sailed away. She knew it was an irrational analogy—Duke hadn't left them to drown, for pity's sake—but she was short on oxygen nevertheless.

"That was my doing," Cabrini said. "I wanted to

be the one to tell you. I've decided to take over this project myself."

"You decided?" Annie closed her hands into fists to stop their trembling. She ordered herself to calm down. Jack Cabrini was the CEO of the company; he must know what he was doing. Duke had always spoken of Cabrini with high praise. He'd even said he'd learned more working for Cabrini than he'd learned from all other bosses he'd had in his career.

"Mr. Cabrini," Tess said, "we—"

"Please, call me Jack."

"Umm, all right. Jack," Tess continued, "we can't, I mean—you've taken us by surprise, and not in a good way. We plunged into this project partly because we could rely on Duke."

"Are you saying you'll be here like Duke was?" Annie asked. "Handling twenty or thirty decisions every day? And still run your whole company?"

The more she thought about it, the less plausible it was and the angrier she became. He might be brilliant, but she couldn't help thinking Jack Cabrini was taking over Albion House like some kind of hobby, a What-I-Did-on-My-Summer-Vacation project.

"Yes," he said, "I'll be here. I've come to Bitter Falls four times to check on progress, but I didn't meet with you. The first time was before we signed the contract. And I've stayed on top of the details, thanks to Duke. From the outset, I've been personally interested in Albion House."

"Maybe we should—" Annie stopped, collected her thoughts. Took a deep breath and exhaled slowly. "Let's go inside out of the sun. Maybe have a glass of wine. Talk this over."

"Thanks. I'd like that," Cabrini said. "And who's this?"

Without Annie noticing, her daughter had approached the three of them, circling so she was mostly behind her mom. As usual, around a man she didn't know, Savannah was shy as the fawns Annie had watched. None of the workmen, except Duke, had succeeded in getting a word out of her.

"This is my daughter, Savannah." Annie smiled at her daughter, trying to telegraph the message: smile, *it's okay, I'm right here*. But Savannah, as usual, rolled her lower lip in and nibbled it. Her blue-green eyes were large, studying the stranger, while she stayed a good ten feet away.

"You must be the girl with the blue and white room," he said. "Did you choose the color?"

She looked at Annie and then back at him, gave a nod.

"Now I see how the trim matches your eyes," he said. "Good choice."

"Savannah," Tess said, "come with me and we'll put out some cookies for Mr. Cabrini." Tess headed for the wide front steps to the wrap-around porch, and Savannah ran to catch up.

Annie wanted to run as well. She'd pass Tess like she was standing still. What an impression that would make. Something about Jack Cabrini interfered with her balance.

"Savannah baked the cookies, with help of course. You'll make her happy if you join us."

"Make her happy" hung in the air, and Annie felt a twinge of guilt for sounding ungracious. Clearly, she should have said that Jack joining "us" would make "us" happy.

"Thanks. I'm a fool for homemade cookies. Ask my little sister, Marcy. She's moving here with me, by the way. You'll see her from time to time."

"Moving here?" Annie asked. "Oh, of course, you'll need to stay for the summer." The ground seemed like a safe place to direct her eyes. Ground, shoes, the bottom of his slacks. When she looked at his eyes, she felt like an oxygen mask should drop down in front of her face.

What a weird combination of emotions flooded

through her. Anger, anxiety at what was at its core a business crisis—not even a true crisis but a setback. And, also, attraction.

She looked at his eyes again and barely managed not to say aloud what she was thinking: *Oh, my God.*

"Not just for the summer."

There was something husky in his voice, something hesitant. She wondered if he was having an oxygen problem, too. *Maybe it's the altitude.*

"I'll explain our plans over wine," he said, "to you and Tess."

As Annie walked up the stairs beside him, she noticed his height, three or four inches over six feet. Perfect for her, even in heels. She felt a wave of heat.

Heat? Where had that blizzard gone? This was like the bizarre Chinook winds she'd heard about. Hot wind rushes down and raises the temperature fifty degrees in an hour. Sap rises so fast it splits trees wide open. Crazy climate.

It was all she could do to keep from fanning herself with her hand. Her sap was rising, all right. Maybe she didn't need therapy. Maybe what she needed was a dose of romance.

The same way a pressure cooker needs a release valve.

Am I insane? I don't even know if he's married or not.

She hesitated at the entrance. *I should say something, but what?*

"I guess I don't have to apologize for the place being a mess, do I?" she asked.

His smile dazzled her like an unexpected spotlight. How many women had succumbed to that smile? No, she didn't want to know.

He held the thick plastic drape away from what would be the entry to the foyer, and Annie ducked her head under his arm. Her sandals made a hollow sound on the plywood that covered the beautiful parquet floor.

In spite of her anxiety over losing Duke as the on-site boss of the project, and in spite of the hormonal storm set off by Jack Cabrini's warm eyes and hot smile, Annie felt a familiar rush of anticipation as she entered Albion House. She'd been involved in dozens of renovations of old homes in Seattle and Portland, but always as a consultant. An employee. She could advise the owners how best to recapture the elegance of eighty to one hundred twenty years ago, but every choice was the owner's decision.

Now, through a bizarre turn of events, she and Tess were holding the reins of a project. Tied to their own past, they were shaping their future.

Jack stopped to look up through the two sets of stairs and multiple landings visible from the entryway.

"Good," he said. "There's more natural light since the crew tore out the wall that blocked off the east end of the third floor. It will be even better when we replace the glass in the windows on that landing."

"It will be a cozy place to sit and read. For us, and the guests, too. I'm thinking the cabinet below the window seat will be a good place to store games."

She realized she'd moved close to him to see from his perspective. She was near enough to smell his aftershave; near enough to see how close he'd shaved. He looked down at her, and a smile played around his lips. A slow, lazy, bedroom smile.

Self-consciously, she stepped back. To have something to do, she smoothed and tightened the canvas covering the banisters and newel posts carved of Honduras mahogany.

"I'm so glad these are intact," she said. "The unique stairway will be the first thing guests notice."

"True. And my guess is that the marble fireplace

will be the second thing they notice."

He stepped into the shell of what had been Goldie's parlor and caressed the stone. Carved in Italy, the fireplace and mantel had come by ship, all the way around Cape Horn, then by land from Portland.

She tried to imagine guests in front of the fireplace, but the picture that flickered in her mind was of a little girl named Savannah and a dog, and a mom reading aloud from Rudyard Kipling. The mansion would be an inn, but it would also be their home.

Tess appeared from the dark walkway that led to the kitchen. "Cookies, anyone?"

"Sounds good to me." Jack straightened up from examining the marble.

"I'll be there in a minute," Annie said.

She watched them walk single file under the open ductwork. Tess talked cheerfully about the rental house they'd found and the farmer's market that was starting on Saturday for the summer and fall.

Tess knew more than she did about turning Albion House into a successful bed and breakfast. She'd majored in hospitality in college, trained with Marriott in San Francisco, and worked as a hotel executive in Seattle, the same career as their father.

But this part of the project, the recreation of a historic home from the basement up, was Annie's great professional and personal love. It was physical and emotional at the same time.

Of course, knowing how to order rare wall coverings and period light fixtures from boutiques in London was not the same as knowing how to tape and mud green board and how to install wiring to an antique chandelier in a twelve-foot ceiling.

No, for that she needed the best general contractor money would buy.

The best. Duke.

She almost moaned aloud. *Stop thinking about that.*

It had been draining to establish good communication with Duke and his crew chiefs. Interface with construction experts was difficult, even on a good day. No one—herself included—could find charm in hundred-year-old plumbing.

What would it be like with a contractor CEO who might disappear at any time to oversee a project worth millions? She'd heard rumors, from friends in Seattle, that Great Western might bid on a skyscraper project in Bellevue. Jack Cabrini's stated "personal interest" in Albion House was probably not worth much.

But doesn't that make getting along with him even more imperative?

She swallowed hard; pride was always hard to swallow. It was time to act like the professional designer she was.

She followed the route Tess and Jack had taken. In a bay window area at the end of the kitchen, Tess had placed a paper plate of peanut butter cookies on a makeshift table, an old door that Duke had set on sawhorses as a work surface.

"Oops," Tess said, "I offered wine before I remembered that we don't have a corkscrew."

Jack pulled a Swiss Army knife out of his pocket and removed the cork from the bottle she'd placed on the table.

"Thanks." Tess smiled and poured the chardonnay into three Dixie cups. "To your health."

"And yours," he said. "And now, I'm going to try one of these cookies."

Annie's "mom vision," with its proverbial third eye, read Savannah's face. Without the guile of adults, who would pretend to have no interest in the cookies, Savannah avidly watched the tall stranger munch the cookie and study the flavor.

Annie pressed one finger to her lips to keep from

chuckling. She'd seen professional wine tasters give less thought to their palates than Jack displayed. At last, he murmured "umm-umm" and displayed his patented dazzler.

Savannah's smile cracked open her face.

"I'll bet these are hard to make," he said. "Could I take one with me for my little sister, Marcy, to taste?"

Savannah nodded, sober as a judge, but with more gravitas. Then she held up two fingers.

"One for Marcy and one more for me? Or two for me and none for Marcy?"

Savannah giggled and shook her head.

"You were going to tell us that you and your sister are moving to Bitter Falls for a while?" Annie prompted.

"Not just for a while. I bought a house three miles out of town, in Coldwater Canyon. We're here to stay."

"That seems like an extreme change," Tess said, "with your company headquartered in Denver."

"I'm in the process of selling Great Western to a consortium. It's too big. I got so I was spending ninety percent of my time with lawyers and accountants. Too far from what I loved doing." He held out his right hand, palm down. "I'm losing my calluses. Time to get back to basics. In fact, I've got my old tool belt out in my truck, the one my dad gave me when I was in high school."

Annie saw Tess, who was slightly behind Jack, cross her eyes and stick her tongue out the corner of her mouth like a cartoon dog at a steak bone. To keep from laughing, Annie had to swing her gaze away to a safer view, to the trucks parked out back. She was sure Tess was imagining, as she was, what Jack Cabrini would look like in low-slung jeans and a tool belt. It was no coincidence that the bare-chested construction guy was Annie's favorite on the Men of Montana calendar. And Tess knew it.

"So, do you plan to live in Bitter Falls year round?" Tess asked. "Everyone we meet warns us how long winter lasts in Montana."

"In fact," Annie added, "their latest barb is that they remember a year it snowed on June first."

"Winter won't scare me off," Jack scoffed. "I'm into winter sports, and mulled wine, and fireplaces. And a stack of good books. I used to love that about Denver, that I could get out to Vail to ski two or three days a week. As the company grew and money came in, I bought a condo at Beaver Creek. But every year I skied less and worked more. Last year I was on the slopes for eight days. Eight." He shook his head. "It was time to ask if I owned the company or it owned me."

Annie nodded. This change to their building project was a lot to absorb, and her wild imagination about tool belts and muscles—and now après-ski by a stone fireplace—wasn't helping her focus.

Mulled wine, indeed. And did he say a stack of good books? Where did this guy come from? Some branch of Make-a-Wish for single women? She took a sip of chardonnay.

"Knowing this project as you do," she said, "I'm wondering, do you think we'll be opening our doors at the end of August? Right now, we don't even *have* doors."

He grinned.

Annie could swear her knees knocked. Jack Cabrini's grin was a deadly weapon.

"It's moving along better than expected," he said. "Duke hired an extra crew of six cement specialists for the next four days to get the garage floors and the solarium sub-floor poured, along with the footings for the hot tub and gazebo. Tomorrow at first light we'll have a massive concrete truck here. And technically, you do have doors. We found a custom door designer in Coeur d'Alene. He'll have them ready in plenty of time."

He answered every question they tossed his way, gave them his cell phone number, and excused himself.

"I'll be here early tomorrow. Call me anytime if you have a question."

Tess gave him the plate with five remaining cookies.

"Thanks," he said. "Marcy is going to want the recipe for these. Would that be all right with you, Savannah? To share your recipe?"

She beamed at his attention and nodded her head. She didn't go so far as to speak to him, but Annie had a feeling that would come, too. CEO Jack Cabrini was winning endorsements from all three of the Rikers.

Life in Bitter Falls, she admitted to herself, just got a lot more interesting.

Chapter Two

Jack waved one more time at the two women and one little girl on the porch of Albion House. Making a tight U-turn, he drove down the hill toward Main Street.

Right now the town could be described as "sleepy," but he'd heard a dozen times that the population would swell with tourists and construction crews after the first of June. Like Whitefish, Montana, and Ketchum, Idaho, Bitter Falls was in the process of being "discovered" by Hollywood. People with money to burn were building second, or—more likely—third or fourth houses in the scenic river valley. Great Western Construction got requests for bids almost daily.

Another reason behind the housing boom in Bitter Falls was a blitz of national publicity seven months ago. The prize, won in federal court, was recovering the patent to a kind of solar cell invented by a man in Bitter Falls, an invention that could revolutionize life for people in the developing nations. The Suncatcher factory had been up and running one month after the late October court decision, and an expansion was in the works.

Great Western hadn't bid on Suncatcher's expansion. Jack had so much work in the pipeline, he didn't want more. That had been true of the Albion House project, too, when the proposal landed on his desk. But there was something about it that called him to get involved.

Called me? He laughed. Maybe the ghost of sad, bitter old Goldie Jones had his cell phone number.

Whatever the catalyst, he'd bid on and won the

contract. And the Albion project had worked like a crowbar to get him out of his deepening rut. The project, and Marcy's trouble, forced him to reevaluate his life.

And he didn't much like what he'd seen.

Time to take a radical left turn. Get off the superhighway and onto a country road.

The way he and his attorneys had structured the sale of Great Western, his new construction company would carve off his favorite kind of construction, custom homes and small multiple-dwelling projects, for the western Montana and northern Idaho region. He had to decide on a name soon. *Blank-Blank* Custom Construction.

It wouldn't be his last name, that was certain. The purpose of this move was to get him off the fame-and-ego grid.

He grinned and waved at a friendly old guy in bib overalls waiting to cross Main Street at one of Bitter Falls' two stoplights.

It was luck on both sides that the Riker sisters had pressed Great Western for a bid a year ago. He'd been in the doldrums, dissatisfied with the career he'd planned on since he was about twelve. No, since he was nine, building his magnificent treehouse. Albion became his new "treehouse" project. Even though he would probably never hammer a nail into it, he could watch and participate from a distance.

At least, that was his thinking during the bidding process and the first eight months of the contract. It was then that the word "sell" crept into his thinking.

He'd had offers to sell Great Western before, but he'd tossed them off his desk. But for some reason, in January, he started studying them, consulting his corporate attorneys, returning phone calls. One offer was too good to dismiss.

More study, more consultation, more phone calls.

Later, when Marcy's trouble shook the two of them and the idea of leaving Denver took over his thinking, he looked down at his desk and saw...Duke Hemmer's weekly update on Albion House. The only paperwork he actually looked forward to.

Worry simply melted off his shoulders.

He'd called his attorney, who called the potential buyers. Once the deal was pounded into shape, he was on a plane to Montana. He found a house to buy and broke the news to Duke Hemmer, insisting on confidentiality.

Today, however, when he'd seen the stricken looks on Annie and Tess Riker's faces, he feared for a moment that he'd made a serious mistake by not making the project handoff gradual.

He sighed. For a moment, hell. He still feared it was a mistake.

Oh well. He'd already done it. As Marcy so often said, with the withering disdain only a teenage girl could carry off, *whatever!* Now job one was to win the confidence of the Riker sisters. He and his assistants at Great Western called this part of the business "massaging the client."

Hmmm. This time the phrase had all sorts of hidden implications. *Erotic* implications.

He'd like to massage Annie Riker all over. With fragrant oil. Work the tension out of her shoulders. Work the tension out of her *whatever.*

The ladies of Albion House. Savannah was adorable, with those magnetic blue-green eyes and wavy blond hair. Tess was friendly, smart, good looking. Easy to talk to.

And then there was Annie. Yowza. The sisters both had blue eyes and light brown hair. Tess wore hers long, but Annie's was short, sort of spiked. It showed her neck to advantage. Her kissable neck.

He swore softly. Slow down, he told himself. She's a client; we'll be working closely for the next three or four months. Four months of intense concentration, long days, and probably a few disagreements.

Keep it professional.

The all-male, all-erogenous part of Jack that had just awakened from a long slumber called him several unprintable and unprofessional names, then settled back to grumpy sleep.

It had been too damn long since he'd been attracted to a woman. Really attracted, not just a dinner date and *whatever.*

His cell phone rang, and he answered without looking at the number. "Hello?"

"Jack, how's it going? How is Marcy adjusting?"

"Pretty good, Travis. Of course it's still a vacation at the dude ranch to Marcy. Real adjustment will come when we move into our house and become bona fide Montana residents."

Actually, even that wouldn't be difficult. The real adjustment would come in September when Marcy started ninth grade at a new high school. He wanted to go in beside her with a cattle prod to protect her from anyone who didn't make her feel welcome.

"How's Bitter Root, or Bitter Gulch, or whatever that place is called?"

Jack parked in front of the small storefront labeled Historical Museum and turned off his engine. Travis McGarry knew perfectly well what the town was called. He'd listened to Jack rhapsodize about it enough times.

"The name is Bitter Falls, on the banks of the Bitter River; a.k.a. paradise. Why? You coming to visit?"

"Someday. Not on my calendar yet. But I do miss you guys."

Travis was Jack's personal attorney and his best friend since the fifth grade. It had been Travis whom Jack had called the night the police contacted him about Marcy. Travis met him in downtown Denver.

"How's Jessica?" Jack hoped he had the name right. Travis had a revolving door policy when it came to girlfriends.

"Jesse, not Jessica. And last I heard she was fine; planning a big wedding in Dallas."

"You dodged another bullet."

"Close call. I'm not as fast on my feet as I used to be."

"But fast enough."

"Exactly. Fast enough. Anyway, I'm dating a true babe now. Name is Willow. Runner up to Miss Nebraska. She's the early-morning anchor for CBS in Denver. Very hot."

"Congratulations. Uh, was there some reason you called, besides the babe report?"

"In fact, yes. The district attorney is threatening to take Cruella to the grand jury."

Jack swore. "Cruella" was the media's nickname for Luella DeBeers. She was the cyber-bullying mother of Marcy's former classmate, Crystal. And the case was all about what Crystal and her mother had done to Marcy.

As long as it remained a juvenile court matter, with Crystal DeBeers and her co-conspirator Heather Janson—both fourteen years old—in legal trouble, Marcy's name was protected. But if the D.A. put Luella on trial, Marcy would have to testify.

"I want this to go away, Travis!"

"I know, I know. I have calls in to everyone I know in the D.A.'s office, including a guy who delivers mail and a guy who does nothing but shred documents."

"You might have better luck at the other end of the train."

"You and I are thinking the same way, buddy. Derail the caboose. I'm having a drink tonight with Vince Safire, the senior partner of Safire, Colt, and Cooper."

"DeBeers's lawyers?"

"Yes."

"What do you think Luella DeBeers wants? I mean, other than angels to proclaim her blessed among women?"

The real question, they both understood, wasn't simply, *What does she want?* It was, *What will she settle for?*

"I don't know. I'll call you tonight."

Jack almost barked that he didn't want Marcy dragged into a media circus, but Travis knew that. No need to state the obvious.

Instead he muttered, "I'll have my phone on."

He snapped it shut and dropped it in his pants pocket.

What was it his dad liked to say? *Don't go looking for trouble. If it's yours, it'll find you soon enough.*

He got out of his truck, locked it with a touch of the fob, and strolled into the museum. He was right on time to meet Vera Stefano. Jack's office administrator ever since he took over Great Western, Vera was here to examine and copy old photos of Albion House.

He found her at a library table with labeled boxes. She was wearing gloves made of thin white cotton and leafing through a scrapbook.

"Jack, I found just what you were looking for."

"As you always do," he said. "Now will you get some rest?"

Vera Stefano rose, slowly, and he winced to think of her bad hip. Bone on bone, that's how the orthopedic surgeon described it.

Vera was sixty-six and technically retired, but she liked to stay involved with his business. The two of them had built it back to a roaring success after his father died. She'd been his right hand in business and a surrogate mother to Marcy.

And, if he were to be scrupulously honest, she'd been a mom to him, too, as he'd grown up without his own mother. There had been times he and his dad weren't speaking—or weren't speaking civilly—and Vera stood amidst them like an island of calm.

When Jack made up his mind to get Marcy out of Denver, getting Vera to slow down and take care of her health was a bonus. There was never a question of leaving her behind.

"Let me see what you found," he said. "Then we'll meet Marcy for dinner. Maybe find a cowboy for you, too."

"Maybe some old banged-up, bow-legged rodeo clown. Or is Gabby Hayes still alive?" Vera leaned on a cane to keep weight off the hip that needed replacement. "Here's a picture of Albion House after the fire in 1924. Did you meet the owners?"

"Oh, yes. And I think you're going to like them."

He knew he did.

"The museum director, Betty Ralston, told me the owners expect a treasure trove of information about Goldie Jones to arrive soon," Vera said. "Of course, Betty's fingers are itching to go through it." Outside, she unlocked her car and lowered herself slowly into the driver's seat.

"What kind of information?" He'd love to know more about certain features of Albion House. Who designed the unique staircase to the second and third floor? Who carved the banisters and newel posts? Was the heavy wood bar in the solarium really from a bordello in Nevada? It was not likely he'd ever know, but such things fascinated him.

"Betty thinks it's letters Goldie Jones wrote to her lawyer in San Francisco, and his answers. She never gave up hope to find her grandson and his daughter. The daughter was the mother of the young women who inherited the estate."

"We'd better get out to the ranch and see what Marcy has been up to."

Before he started his engine, he took a quick look at the copy of the 1924 photo. It presented an angle he hadn't seen. The back of the mansion and the west end was wreckage. The chimney where the fire started, in what was then a kitchen with servant quarters above it, was a mound of bricks.

In reconstruction, the Queen Anne style vanquished the mish-mash of gothic and Italianate features, and the place began to look attractive. What little was left of the second floor on the west end was left off in favor of a single-story solarium with windows in an arc of almost one hundred eighty degrees.

At the same time, the kitchen was relocated to an addition on the back of the house, and the servants had rooms above that. The kitchen and bathrooms were remodeled, again, after 1950.

The solarium was Albion House's best feature. It would be perfect for the inn's breakfast room, and also an evening wine and cheese room. The rest of the house, with its two turrets and narrow, gabled rooms on the abbreviated third floor, was getting a much-needed infusion of light and cheerfulness.

Fifteen minutes later, Jack drove through the massive log entrance to the Rocking Star Guest Ranch and found a shady place to park. He powered down the windows while he waited for Vera. She was only a few minutes behind him.

When he'd left the ranch, at three o'clock, Marcy had been in love with a boy from New Orleans. Garrett, was that his name? Fifteen. An older man to thirteen-year-old Marcy. Six feet tall, probably one hundred twenty pounds—and that was counting his braces.

Last night she'd fallen in love with Rusty the horse wrangler, but Jack said if he heard one more word about Rusty, who was about twenty-five, they'd check out of the ranch and sleep on the floor of their house. Garrett the beanpole was more her speed. And more guests would arrive tomorrow morning, so who knew? A new McDreamy might leave Garrett at the starting line.

He sighed. He'd wanted *normal,* and apparently this was it. People who defined this merry-go-round as normal also said raising a teenager would turn his hair gray before he was forty. If that was true, he had a little more than six dark-haired months to go.

He and Marcy were all the family either of them had. When his father and much-younger stepmother died in the crash of a small airplane, Jack had been twenty-eight.

The prodigal son, that's what Ace Cabrini had called him. Jack must have heard that from a dozen people at the funeral.

The prodigal son. But Jack never had the chance to repent, and Ace never had the chance to roast the fatted calf.

Repentance, when it came, was too damn late.

After his mom died, when Jack was eleven, he'd grown up close to his dad. Well, close in some ways. The two of them had locked horns on too many occasions.

But the friction was on personal matters, not on the job. From Ace, Jack had learned the construction business from the dirt up. He'd gone to the University of Colorado, earning a degree in architecture while having the advantage of practical knowledge of construction. He'd been ready to join his dad as partner in Great Western when Ace married beautiful young Beatrice. They'd been married about ten minutes when Ace announced, proudly, at the wedding reception, that Beatrice was pregnant.

Jack had returned to his dad's house only long enough to pack a suitcase and pick up his passport. He'd thrown the keys to his car, a graduation present from Ace, on the kitchen counter, and left for Europe.

All he'd needed to live yacht to yacht and guesthouse to townhouse was his looks and wit. For two and a half years he'd polished his Italian and learned more about classic architecture while living *la dolce vita.*

The extravagance and laughter had ended with one phone call. In Cannes for the film festival, at dinner with a pouty-lipped starlet with perfect breast implants, Jack could barely make out Vera's words through her choking sobs.

He'd returned to Denver to bury his father and Beatrice and take guardianship of a two-year-old girl he'd never seen. As if that wasn't tough enough, he'd discovered that Great Western Construction was a victim of a massive credit swindle that was shaking Colorado to its rocky foundations.

With Vera's help, and his reservoir of know-how, he'd resurrected Great Western. From the sub-basement up.

Ditto for himself. CEO, friend of the governor, escort—and occasionally lover—of rich, beautiful women. Even some flattering pressure to run for the U.S. Congress.

Vera pulled her Ford sedan in beside his truck; she'd driven a truck herself for years but had to buy a sedan when her hip got so bad. He powered up the windows, then had to chase a fly out the door instead. He liked horses, but he hated flies.

He got out, draped his sports coat over his shoulder with one finger, and locked the truck doors with a click.

"Something smells good." Vera sniffed the air as she took his arm.

Annie Riker smells good. He'd noticed her scent when they stood so close in the foyer of Albion House. Floral, fresh. Tempting.

"Barbecued chicken and ribs," he said, telling himself to stay on topic. "I saw the menu posted before I left. Let's find Marcy and get a table."

"Jack! Aunt Vera!" Marcy called from across the grassy lawn. Sprinklers fanned back and forth.

Vera laughed. "It's so good to see her grow up happy and self-confident. Your dad and Beatrice would be proud of her—and proud of the job you've done."

"Thirteen and three-quarters is a long way from grown up." The years ahead yawned like a chasm in front of him, but it was infinitely better to face the years here, in a small town, than in Denver. Better to be close by, not out of town for one or two weeks out of every month.

Marcy met them at the edge of the patio. She was wearing black Wranglers jeans and a white cowboy shirt fringed with black.

"Jack," she said with a giggle of delight, "Garrett wants me to go to the movie with him and his mom and dad. Can I? I mean, may I?"

He gave her the "Who? When? What time? What movie?" quiz and sighed. "Okay, but when you get back to the ranch, you come straight to the cabin."

"Why?"

"Because I'm jealous," he muttered. "We moved here so we could spend more time together, and I've hardly seen you."

"I'll go tell Garrett!" She was gone.

"Get used to this," Vera said. "Her exuberance is proof that you're doing a good job."

"You mean, the better I'm doing as a dad, the less I'll see of her? Somehow that doesn't add up."

"That's how it works. I had this same conversation with your dad when you were fourteen and wanted to spend a year as an exchange student in France."

"I almost died of homesickness."

She laughed. "You managed to hide it well. All we heard was what a wonderful time you were having."

He stiffened his arm to help her up the steps of the lodge. "I had to protect my pride. Nothing would make me admit I hated the school, hated France, and wished I were back in Denver."

She walked ahead of him into the lodge and headed for the dining room. "The time apart was good for both of you. Sometimes the most important lessons have to bite you in the butt."

He wondered if "bite *you*" was a generic, all-purpose *you*, applicable to all, or if she meant, specifically, that Jack Cabrini needed such a lesson. He frowned, deciding he didn't want to know the answer.

"I'll go through the buffet line," he said. "Would you prefer chicken or ribs?"

"A small piece of chicken. Thanks, Jack."

He stopped on the way for Marcy to introduce him to Garrett and his parents. They assured him they'd be in the theater with "the kids" and they'd have Marcy home by ten.

It all made him feel like an old fogey. Which he kind of was. He emphasized that he was her brother, not her dad, partly because he preferred to think he wasn't old enough to have a kid her age. But, hey. Do the math. Marcy was born when he was twenty-six.

If he were to have a kid of his own, soon, he was already old enough to be in the group labeled "mature first-time parents."

Yeah. And if he didn't get married and have a kid soon, he'd be in the group labeled "fathers of infants, easily mistaken for grandfathers."

Such mental meandering, while his hands were busy dishing up two plates at the western buffet, led him—inevitably—to Annie Riker and her kissable neck.

Attracted to a client. So not a good thing.

He returned to the table, pleased that Marcy had joined them without his asking. He was taking Vera's advice, giving her more freedom. It was hard to do. Partly it was hard because he'd been a teenage boy himself. A long time ago.

Okay, a long, long time ago.
But some things don't change.

He cut up his chicken breast and baked potato and dipped the chicken in barbecue sauce as he ate it.

Thank goodness Marcy had a good head on her shoulders. She'd proven that, in living color and three dimensions, in Denver. He wasn't sure he'd have had the moxie to stand up to Crystal DeBeers and Heather Janson.

As for standing up to Cruella DeBeers, he hoped it wouldn't come to that. But Marcy had told him she'd do it if she had to.

The two of them had a lot of hope riding on Travis's powers of persuasion and coercion.

"Before you leave for the movie," he said, "I want you to sample some cookies I brought from Albion House. They were made, with help, by a little girl named Savannah. I want to phone this evening and tell her how much you love them and how you want the recipe."

"It sounds to me like you've already decided what to say." Marcy grinned and licked the sauce off her fingers.

"Mostly, yeah. But I'd rather be telling the truth."

"You've already tasted them?" Vera asked.

"Sure. And they're good. Peanut butter, my favorite."

"How old is the girl?" Marcy spoke to him, but her attention was on a rowdy bunch that came in and couldn't find a table.

Jack recognized them from breakfast. A blended family who were having a lot of trouble adjusting to living together. The dad—and now stepdad—confided to Jack in the lobby that going on vacation together had been unwise.

They separated into two groups and found space. He saw the mom and dad look at each other, wistfully, across the room.

"Savannah is five," he answered. "She's an only child. Very quiet. She reminds me of you at that age. I used to have to peel you off me at the daycare center."

"Reminds you of me, huh? So, she's beautiful, smart, talented."

"And did I mention, quiet?"

She wiped her sticky hands on the napkin. "I've got to go to the cabin and brush my teeth. I probably have strings of beef hanging like ornaments."

"Let me see," Vera said.

Marcy gave a big, closed-teeth smile.

"Wow. You might want to save some of that for lunch tomorrow," Jack said. "Along with the lettuce there on the left."

Marcy whacked him with her cloth napkin. "I've got to hurry. It's almost time to leave for the movie."

He laid his napkin beside his plate and rose. "I'll go get the cookies and meet you at the cabin."

Marcy smiled, this time keeping her lips closed. "Does this little girl, by chance, have a pretty mother?"

He shrugged. "She has a mother, yes. And now that I think about it, she's not half ugly."

"I'll meet you at the cabin. See you tomorrow, Aunt Vera."

"Have fun."

"I'll be back in a little while," Jack said.

"Not on my account," Vera answered. "I'm going straight home. I like my quiet house."

She leaned on the table for support as she stood and centered her weight. Automatically, Jack moved to her side and offered his arm.

"I'll walk you out. By the way, has the surgeon's office called you yet?"

"I was about to tell you. My blood work is back, and my surgery is set for July fifth."

"I can be—"

"You can be nothing," she said. "My sister is coming from Denver. She'll do for me. Same as I did for her last year. You may send me a lavish bouquet, however, and visit the hospital so all the nurses will be ga-ga and give me special attention."

They went down the lodge steps slowly and picked up speed on the straightaway. As soon as Vera pulled her sedan out of the parking lot, Jack retrieved the cookies and strode, quickly, toward his cabin.

He was glad of several things this first day at the head of his new, smaller, as yet unnamed company. Right now, he was glad he'd have an excuse, in a few minutes, to call Annie Riker.

His phone rang, and he scooped it out of his pocket. Caller ID showed it was Travis.

"What do you hear?"

"Don't get your hopes too high, Jack. Vince Safire doesn't take the district attorney's threat against Luella DeBeers seriously. That means he won't look for a deal."

Jack understood what that meant. It was more likely the case would end up in court—with Marcy in the witness chair, and her face pasted all over the internet.

"Safire blew off everything I said," Travis continued. "He says it's a piss-ant case and the D.A. 'doesn't have the balls' to prosecute Luella."

"That stinks."

"True, but it's only a setback. Derailing the train from the back didn't work, so I'll have to be more aggressive about talking to the guys in the locomotive."

"I hope—never mind. You know what I hope. Call me as soon as you know something."

"Will do. Give my love to Marcy."

Chapter Three

On Tuesday morning, Annie poured milk from the gallon jug into a pint measuring cup with a handy spout. Savannah wanted to pour milk on her cereal "by mine own self." This intermediate step saved a lot of clean up.

Her blond hair was in two high ponytails, each wrapped in a tight roller to give them a little curl.

"Is Mr. Cabrini's sister gonna come today?" Savannah poured the milk with the delicacy of a research chemist.

"He didn't say if she would come today. We'll have to wait and see." She removed the rollers and twirled the silky curls around her finger.

Savannah had speculated from suppertime Monday until bedtime on the age of Mr. Cabrini's little sister, pressing Annie and Tess for their guesses. Annie picked sixteen because it was a round number.

Tess picked twenty—but murmured to Annie that a man his age probably has a sister who's about thirty.

"Technically," she added, "I'm *your* little sister."

Annie was glad to see her response time with a dish towel to her *little* sister's butt was still fast.

Savannah picked six because six would be more fun.

Annie had winced, fearing Savannah would be disappointed. She needed playmates, but it was hard to meet kids. They'd arrived too late for her to enroll in a preschool class. True, she'd meet lots of kids in September, when she started kindergarten, but that was a long way off.

At bedtime, Annie had dried Savannah's hair with a towel and helped her into her Snow White nightgown.

"I hope Mister Cabrini's little sister is six or seven or eight." She'd kissed the nose of Missy Mermaid, her favorite sleeping companion.

Annie tucked the sheet around her and kissed her cheeks and forehead. Was any fragrance on earth as sweet as a little girl's clean, damp hair?

"It could be fun if Marcy's older, too," she suggested. "Maybe she knows how to do cartwheels."

Savannah's eyes widened at that possibility, as if she were seeing herself learning that most amazing of tricks, the cartwheel, and moving on to what was clearly the next step, the circus trapeze.

Expectations for Mister Cabrini's sister were running far ahead of reality. Unpleasant scenarios played in Annie's mind, that the girl might be a surly teenager who would want nothing to do with a lonely five-year-old girl. Savannah would be so hurt.

That was the "down" side of motherhood. Not only did she feel the sting of anything that hurt her personally, like sniping from a business associate having a bad day, or a client who denied she'd ordered the color that arrived, but she felt every pinprick of disappointment her child felt.

If a woman had a husband to talk to, someone who loved their child...

But she didn't, so she might as well stop thinking, "What if...?"

Good advice. Excellent advice.

Still, as Annie closed her daughter's bedroom door, she longed for the best thing a good marriage had to offer. Stated simply, *Trouble shared is halved; joy shared is doubled.*

Now, in the blazing bright morning sun, Annie cut up a nectarine and gave it, along with a napkin, to Savannah. She said nothing more about Cabrini's sister, changing the subject instead to adding a set of plastic dishes to Savannah's playhouse.

Changing the subject inside her head was not so easy. She was loath to admit it, but her expectations regarding Mr. Cabrini himself were galloping toward the horizon, reins flying. Where did such thoughts come from? And it wasn't just *thoughts*. Her body was in open rebellion to her sensible mind.

She wanted Jackson T. Cabrini's arms around her, which was utterly ridiculous. *Am I deprived, or depraved? Or a little of both?*

She tried to think of ten good reasons she should not go to Albion House and see him today.

Okay, nine. Eight?

She could only think of one.

Because I'll make a fool of myself, staring at him with impossible-to-deny lust.

Through the open front door she heard the sound of a car stopping. She walked to the living room in time to see the postman, in blue walking shorts, hoist himself out of the red, white, and blue Jeep.

"Good morning," he called.

She opened the screen and waited on the small front porch.

"You're mighty early."

"Oh, this isn't part of my route. I'll be back again around lunchtime to walk the street. This here is special delivery. Two, in fact."

He held a white cardboard box, a cube about fourteen inches on a side, with bright Special Delivery stickers on it.

"Here you go," he said.

"Ooof," Annie muttered. "It's heavy." She set it on the porch swing so she could sign the delivery receipt.

"Now, where is—? Oh, I must have left it on the front seat. I'll be right back."

While he hurried back to the Jeep and returned to the porch, she examined the return label on the box. As she expected, it was from Dusart and Dusart, Attorneys at Law, in San Francisco. It had been a registered letter from that firm that had changed her life, and Tess's, fifteen months ago.

This had to be the years of accumulated correspondence between Goldie and her lawyers, the record of her search for her grandson and then for her great-granddaughter. The current senior partner bearing the name Dusart was a great-grandson of Leopold Dusart, Goldie's lawyer when she was young and rich and living in San Francisco, at the turn of the last century.

Riley Dusart had promised Annie and Tess that he would find the correspondence and the chronological reports of the detective agencies they'd employed over the years.

"Here it is," the postman said. "Sorry for the delay."

Again she signed the receipt and thanked him.

"How are things coming along at Albion House?"

"Good," she said. "Every day is a new adventure."

"Well, you have a fine day now."

She wished him the same as she studied the envelope. It, too, was from a law firm. This one was in Seattle. Chenoweth, Chenoweth, followed by—she counted—four more names. The box was addressed to both her and Tess; this one was only to her.

The name Chenoweth was like a finger down her throat. *Gag!* Six years ago she'd sat in a Seattle courtroom and watched the second one, Isaac, son of the late Trammel C. Chenoweth, in action.

Isaac Chenoweth, Vermin at Law.

She took the box and letter inside and half-listened to Savannah's long story about the lilac playhouse. She was an imaginative child, used to playing alone. Living as an only child with a mom and an aunt, and spending quite a bit of time with a grandpa she adored, she'd developed the vocabulary of an older child, but she was painfully shy with strangers. Even with children her own age she was slow to relax and be herself.

Annie's dad, Paul Riker, said she'd been the same way as a child. She smiled and reminded herself to call him around noon. He was certainly dragging his feet on his retirement and his move to Montana.

She slit open the envelope with a steak knife and pulled out two pages.

Contacting you on behalf of our client, Sheldon Roth...

"Oh, sh—sugar," she said, remembering in time that Savannah was nearby. Her skin went cold and clammy, and her blood rushed to her core, leaving her lightheaded.

During his incarceration, Mr. Roth received three letters from your attorney, Delia Phinney, requesting that he sign a document terminating his parental rights to his daughter, Savannah Jane Riker.

As you know, he did not answer those letters.

Now, due to unusual circumstances, Mr. Roth's ten-year sentence has been commuted, and today he is being released from federal custody. He plans to move out of the United States and get a fresh start.

Before he makes that permanent move, he plans to sign the document you have requested. We have the termination of parental rights document here at our office. However, he will not sign it until he meets his daughter. He says to assure you he will not tell her he is her father.

Please advise Mr. Roth, through us, when he can meet Savannah Jane Riker. The sooner the meeting takes place, in Montana or Seattle, the sooner the document will be signed.

A copy of this letter is being sent, also by Special Delivery, to your attorney of record, Delia Phinney.

Thank you for your prompt response, Ms. Riker.

"Mommy, can I? I mean, may I?"

"I'm sorry, sweetheart. I was reading something and I—I didn't hear what you said."

"May I invite Marcy to the lilac playhouse?"

"Oh, sweetheart...I don't know. We'll talk about it this afternoon."

Annie's heart ached to see how lonely Savannah was. One mention of a "little sister" named Marcy and she'd constructed an entire fantasyland of fun and friendship.

And I'm doing the same damn thing with Jack Cabrini!

Sudden clarity pierced her like a laser beam. She knew less than nothing about Jack Cabrini, and she was building a myth. It wasn't about Jack and whether he was smart, fun, sexy or kind. It was about *her need.* It was about what *she wanted* in her life.

Okay, she told herself. Time to cowboy up, to ride until the buzzer sounds. For once, go for total honesty.

Face the *déjà vu.* Look it square in the eye.

Marrying Peter Dylan was all about my need, about what I wanted in my life. The whirlwind romance and sudden wedding in Hawaii was the story I, Annie Riker, had been writing in my head ever since I put on big girl pants.

"Mommy, when can we get our puppy?"

"I already answered you about the puppy. Not until we move into Albion House. Hey, did you make your bed?"

Savannah looked at the ceiling as if the answer hovered in the air. "I think I did. I'll go look."

Annie poured a cup of coffee, added half and half, and sipped. The sound of the shower stopped in the bathroom. She hated to show this letter to Tess.

No, she shouldn't be so negative. Once Tess got past the initial shock, she'd see, as Annie did now, that it was good news. The man Annie had known as Peter Dylan—and "loved," as pathetic as that was in light of all she'd later learned—would be out of their lives forever. Soon. She only had to live through the nauseating experience of seeing him one more time. Seattle, or Montana? Definitely Seattle. She didn't want him to pollute Montana by setting foot across the state line.

Savannah came back to the table and continued to peel the crust off her toast.

Annie folded the letter and placed it in the envelope. She would talk to Tess, then call Delia, then call her dad. The quicker she ripped the bandage off, the sooner she'd feel better.

"Hello, hello, hello!"

"Grandpa!" Savannah hopped off her chair and raced to the front screen door. In two seconds she had her arms wrapped tight around Paul Riker's neck.

"Stop, stop, you're squeezing me into jelly." He crossed his eyes and let his tongue hang out.

Savannah, predictably, had a giggling fit. He danced her around the room.

"Dad," Annie said, "why didn't you tell us you were coming?"

She and Tess had pressed him a dozen times to come see the progress, but his work at the boutique hotel in Seattle, where he was general manager, kept getting in the way. He couldn't leave the hotel's owner, dowager of an old Seattle family, in the lurch, could he?

Lately, she'd wondered if he'd even broken the news to Mrs. Follett that he was going to retire and move to Montana. She and Tess also suspected that his new girlfriend, Giselle, might be keeping him tethered to Seattle more than any devotion to his employer.

He'd introduced Giselle to his daughters in January at a steakhouse in downtown Seattle. When the uncomfortable meal ended, he left to drive Giselle home.

"Do the math," Tess had said to Annie. "No, really, do the math. She's half the age Mother was when she died."

Annie had given a derisive snort. "She's about the half the woman Mother was."

Tess had handed her a napkin. "You've got cream on your whiskers, my dear."

"Mee-ow."

"Dad!" Tess exclaimed as she came out of the bathroom wearing a robe; her hair was wrapped in a towel. "Dad! We've all missed you so much."

"How long can you stay?" Annie asked. "Hurry, get dressed, Tess, so we can show him the house."

Thirty minutes later, they arrived in back of Albion House. As Jack had warned them, action centered on an enormous cement truck with a long tube feeding the cement onto the floor of the seven-car garage.

Like worker bees servicing the queen, men in hardhats smoothed the wet cement and guided the tube to the next spot on the grid.

Annie tore her gaze away from Jack Cabrini, who'd given her a smile and a wave, and followed her family into the kitchen-to-be. Tess was rattling off facts and figures as she set the big silver coffee carafes on the work table. She'd taken to making the coffee extra strong for the men.

Paul cleared his throat and looked at his watch. Cleared it again.

Annie watched him. Something was up.

"I can only stay an hour." Again he looked at his watch, as if it might, inexplicably, display a different time than he'd just seen.

"Come see my playhouse," Savannah chirped, unaware of the tension doubling, quadrupling, filling the room. "This way, come with me, Grandpa."

"Savannah," Annie said, "hold on, sweetheart.

You go set up the tea party. Grandpa will be there in a couple minutes."

Savannah skipped out the side door, her descant monologue undeterred by lack of ears to hear it.

Silence hung in the room. Annie had no intention of breaking it. Was he ill? Was he here to give them bad news, like the day Mom—

No. Don't even begin to think about that day.

"I can only stay an hour," he said again. "I didn't want to tell you this on the phone."

Tess nodded and wet her lips. "We're listening."

Annie's lungs compressed. Pain radiated along her collarbone and up the left side of her neck. She was familiar with the syndrome. Anxiety attack. It was inconvenient, unpleasant, but nothing to worry about.

"I've decided not to move to Montana."

They waited. Annie heard the rumble of the cement truck and the loud beep that meant it was backing up.

"I know I said I wanted to retire, but…I'm not ready to. I'm not ready to leave Seattle. In fact—" here he smiled ruefully, his best naughty-but-loveable-boy smile, "in fact, I'll probably never leave Seattle."

Annie stole a look at Tess; her sister's lips were clamped tight, and her arms were a mirror image of her own, folded rigidly against her waist.

"How is Giselle?" Annie asked. She tried not to sound snarky, but she wasn't snark-proof. Not now. Not when the only father figure her young daughter had ever known—the only man in the world who could lift that precious little girl into the air and squeeze her into jelly—not when that man said he would probably never live in the same state as that little girl again.

He grinned and gave a little shuffle. A stupid, self-centered little "oh shucks" shuffle. It was a social device that worked well on old ladies.

"There's no way to say this except to say it. Giselle and I got married in Vegas. Saturday. She flew straight home today, and I made a detour to Missoula and rented a car."

"If it's true that you have one hour to spend here," Annie said, fighting the urge to hyperventilate, "please spend it with Savannah."

Before tears spilled out of her eyes, she turned and walked woodenly toward the stairs. At the line between the kitchen and the hall, she stopped but didn't turn around.

"Tess, I'll be in the attic. Jack Cabrini called last night and said he'd get here early to..." She pressed the fingers of her right hand against her left collarbone. "He said he would tear out the false wall so I can see if any of the furniture is worth salvaging."

"Be sure to—" Tess cleared her throat. "Be sure to wear gloves. It's spider-ville up there."

"I will."

Instead of the attic, she went to the window bench on the landing of the third floor. From this nook she didn't see the bustling construction project. The view was to the south. Over the river and through the woods.

"No," she whimpered. "If I went over the river..."

The words evaporated in the stale, dry air of the old mansion. Because "over the river and through the woods," as any fool knows, is the way to Grandmother's house.

And Grandmother—Mom—Diana—is dead.

She and Savannah and Tess wouldn't be visiting Giselle for a Norman Rockwell all-American Thanksgiving meal, would they?

Norman Rockwell is dead, too.

Hell, he was probably dead before Giselle was born.

Although—Annie couldn't help but smile at the thought—if they made the holiday schlep to Seattle, it would be delightful for her, and for Tess, to watch Giselle's porcelain complexion and perfect Betty Boop mouth when Savannah called out, "Hi, Gran-maw!"

At last she sighed and stretched. Attic spiders and mice fit pretty well with her mood. Bats would be good, too. She went down one floor to the landing where they kept extra hardhats and other supplies. Suited up in overalls to protect her yellow slacks and blouse, with garden gloves in one pocket and a flashlight in another, she surveyed the tools. She'd come back and get something if she needed it.

She traded her yellow sandals for old running shoes stained with whatever color she'd used on the deck of her last paid project.

This might be an exercise in futility. She hoped, of course, to discover an exquisite piece of furniture, something from Goldie's years in San Francisco, after the Klondike and before Bitter Falls. Reality was probably finding ratty old suitcases left by the maids who worked at Albion House only until they could get a better job. A job where "the mistress" wasn't more bitter than the river, falls and valley she'd chosen as home.

In a bedroom on the third floor, she steadied the ladder Jack said he'd left up there for her. He must have been there long before six o'clock to work in the attic, because he'd mentioned that the truck and crew were to arrive at six-thirty.

At the top of the ladder, Annie put on her gloves and pulled herself up to Spider-ville. Watching where she put her feet, fearing rusty nails more than spiders, she crab-walked along the sloping roof to the vast central space where she could stand up straight. At a screened opening at one end, a ventilation space about two feet square, she heard the cheeping of baby birds. All along the eaves, she knew, were nests of barn swallows.

Duke had promised to disturb them as little as

possible with the reconstruction of gutters and downspouts and with painting. She'd better mention it to Jack.

Realistically, the nests had to go. They couldn't very well paint over or around them. But Duke assured her the job could wait until the baby birds fledged.

The swallow diaspora wouldn't be permanent. New nests would appear when moms needed them. Moms—and dads? Did male barn swallows nurture their young? She'd have to look it up.

She pulled the string on the bare light bulb; she'd replaced it last time she was up here. Now she could see where Jack had ripped a plywood screen, sort of a lean-to wall, away from a storage area. The plywood lay in pieces on the floor. It probably disintegrated when he pulled it away from the rafters.

The light bulb didn't do much for the pile of discarded rugs and furniture. She turned on the flashlight and began gingerly pulling out the items.

One lamp, another lamp. Carpet runners. Moth-eaten draperies. Suitcases, all empty. Lamps. More lamps.

She laughed. She'd unearthed a lamp graveyard. But none of them were valuable. No hidden Louis Comfort Tiffany treasures.

Everything seemed to date to the same period, around World War II. A newspaper lining a dresser drawer confirmed that guess. The Allies were liberating Paris. War raged on in the Pacific.

Goldie would have been seventy-two in the last year of the war. Her only son, Stanley, would have been thirty-seven; he died at age thirty-nine, leaving his widow, Greta, and one surviving son. His second son, born in 1942, had died in infancy.

It had been his marriage to Greta that so angered his mother that she disinherited him. Or, rather, she had her lawyer tell Stanley he wouldn't get a nickel. She left him in her will, believing right up until he died—so long before she did—that he'd come crawling back.

Stanley's first son, Luke, born in 1940, was Annie's grandfather. He'd never known it. He may not have known that he had a daughter. He certainly never took responsibility.

In a classic case of irony, Luke never knew he was the grandson of Goldie Jones, either. Greta, who had been so dreadfully maligned by Goldie, and who had suffered poverty and illness all her life, wouldn't speak of Stanley's mother.

And yet, Luke had been born to adventure. Unlike his parents in every way, Luke was a direct throwback to Goldie. How that must have clawed at Greta's heart.

He'd worked in Alaska as a fisherman, then as a deckhand on freighters. He'd fathered a daughter in San Francisco in 1960, apparently with no more thought than a tomcat, and had gone to South Africa to live out the second half of his life.

Annie wondered, as she had ever since she'd learned of the existence of Luke Jones, whether he'd ever set eyes on her mother. He hadn't left the country until after her birth, but the adoptive parents took her home from the hospital. So it was unlikely.

What kind of man—?

She shrugged off the question. Because "*What kind of woman?*" had no easy answer, either. Goldie Jones had reaped what she'd sown.

If Annie could meet her forbears, she'd skip Luke Jones and Goldie Jones. The heroine in the tale was Greta, the "dance hall floozy" with whom weak Stanley Jones had fallen in love. Not terribly long after King Edward VIII abdicated the throne of England to marry the woman he loved, Stanley stood up to his mother's demand that he come back to Montana and make a suitable match. Instead he married Greta.

And therein lay the tale that led to Annie sitting in the attic of a mansion she and her sister owned. Sitting in the attic...moping.

Stewing in anger at her father, and at Peter Dylan, and the ghost of Goldie Jones. And maybe there was a sliver of anger at herself, but not enough to make her get up and find her dad before he left. Tess would keep a close watch on Savannah as long as Annie hid out, but she had to be hurting, too.

I'll go down in a few minutes.

Her nose wrinkled and crinkled. "Ka-chew!" All the dust she'd stirred up was getting to her.

"Hello?" A man's voice. Her dad?

"I'm up here." She watched as hands appeared at the top of the ladder. Her heart fluttered when Jack Cabrini's face showed above the level of the floor.

"Did you find any gold nuggets Goldie hid from the IRS?"

"Not even gold dust. Just dust-dust."

He bent at the waist and moved toward her. "Any ghosts, friendly or otherwise?"

She thought about the question. Did thinking about long-dead people count? "No. At least, none I could identify."

He folded his tall, athletic body and sat cross-legged beside her. "I met your father as he was leaving. Savannah had her arms around his neck like a tourniquet. Tess peeled her off."

"Did Tess—did she tell you anything?"

"What I could hear, over Savannah's crying, was that he surprised you with wedding news. And you're not throwing a reception."

"I should get down there. Poor Savannah—"

Jack put out his hand and kept her from pushing herself upright.

"Tess has her calmed down. They're out in the playhouse. She asked me to come tell you he's gone."

She exhaled, and exhaled, and exhaled. Who knew she had that much air in her? "Thank you."

"I've had some experience with this." He smiled. "My mom died when I was eleven. When I was twenty-six, no, twenty-five, my dad married a beautiful young woman. Beatrice was a year younger than I was."

"Wow."

"Yeah. I did my best to 'man up,' partly thanks to Dad's administrative assistant, Vera Stefano. She'd been with the company since Dad got it started, and she'd mothered me ever since I'd lost my mom. Vera nagged me to do the right thing and stand up with my dad at the wedding. It was torture, but I did it."

He paused. "The company was big by then, and I was out of graduate school. I figured I'd run projects that kept me away from Denver and the lovebirds. All I had to do was survive the wedding without getting drunk and embarrassing myself."

"Something tells me..." she said.

"The wedding wasn't so bad. But the reception was a bitch."

"Don't stop now." She laughed. "You have my undivided attention."

"My dad, Ace Cabrini, made a treacly sweet toast to his bride. I stifled my gag reflex, lifted my glass—and he announced to one and all that he would be a father in six months."

She said nothing for a moment. "If you came here to cheer me up by pointing out that I could, in a few months or a year, become the half-sister to an infant, your faith in my good nature is sadly misplaced."

"I figured, misery loves company."

"You're not miserable."

"Well, not anymore. That's the point."

She thought it over. "I appreciate you coming up here."

Neither of them said anything; the silence cloaked them. She noticed the dust motes drifting toward the ventilation hole.

"I have a question," he said. "You can probably guess what it is."

The tone of his voice made it clear that it was a personal question.

"My marital status?"

He nodded. "I'm single. Never married."

"I'm single, too," she said. "As to whether or not I was married..." She smiled, but she could feel the familiar stab below her left collarbone. That was exactly how she'd described it the first time it happened. A sensation of being stabbed. Repeatedly. She had tiny pills to take at the onset of an anxiety attack, but of course she didn't have them with her.

"As to whether..." she began again. Stopped. Took a deep breath. "I thought I was married, but it was fraudulent. He was a bigamist."

"How long? How long until you knew?"

"Four months. We weren't together all that time, though. Enough to conceive Savannah." She sniffed back the runny nose and fiercely wiped her eyes with the back of her arm. "I never bring it up, but when clients or casual friends ask that question, I say that I 'was married' and leave it at that. They assume, incorrectly, that I am divorced. They deduce, correctly, that I don't want to talk about it."

"Does he play any part in Savannah's life? No, wait. That was badly phrased. From what you say, playing a part was all he did. To you and at least one other woman."

She nodded. "Two other women. He took more than their self respect, though. He took them, and at least thirty-two well-heeled investors, for two hundred million dollars. So, to answer your question, no, he's played no part in Savannah's life. He's been in federal prison since before she was born."

She crossed her arms over her knees and rested

her forehead on them. The crushing weight of her current dilemma nauseated her. In a few hours she had to tell her attorney how to answer Peter's attorney. In a few days, she'd have to look the son of a bitch in the eye. She'd have to stand there and expose Savannah to the risk of her biological father saying something that might scar her for life.

"Annie, I'd like to see you tonight," Jack said.

"See...me?" She dragged her thoughts back from the quicksand and let Jack's words roll around inside her like the words to a song. She wondered if there was some way she could be misreading his statement. No, no. He couldn't mean anything but that simple wish to...*see me tonight.*

She shook herself out of her reverie and took a deep breath. Slowly, she raised her head and studied his face.

"Tonight? Oh. That's very—I'd like to, but—I can't leave Savannah. She's suffered a tremendous disappointment. I know she's too young to understand the implications, long-term. But she asks us every single day when Grandpa is coming. He's the only man she's ever had in her life."

"Ah, I have a better idea. Even though being alone with you is a hard notion to improve on. How about the three of you join Marcy and me for dinner at the Rocking Star? As long as I call by noon, I can have as many guests as I care to."

"Savannah would love that. Yes. Thank you."

"*Savannah* would love it?" His eyes crinkled at the corners, and he cocked his head, bemused.

"Sorry, that was not gracefully expressed. I'll try again." She held up her right hand. "Mr. Cabrini, I, Annie Riker, would love to meet you and Marcy for dinner. Savannah and Tess will enjoy it, too."

"Much better. Let's meet at the ranch at five o'clock and have time to swim before dinner."

"You're very good at lifting this cloud of self-pity off my shoulders."

He stood and held out his hand. As she got to her feet, sudden cramping behind her right knee combined with sleep-needles in her left foot, and she lost her balance.

When he reached out to steady her, she fell against him, face first against his chest.

"Foot went to sleep," she mumbled into his shirt. "Feels like pins and needles." With him supporting her shoulders, she hopped on one foot until the prickly needles stopped burning.

She looked up at his face, prepared to lie and say she was sorry she'd fallen into his arms. But one look at his eyes and she was speechless.

Softly, without a word, he leaned toward her and kissed the outer corners of her eyes. It was amazingly sensuous.

She tipped her head back and opened her lips. He took the hint. She closed her eyes.

But his kiss was so soft, she wasn't sure their lips really touched. As fired up as she was, as electrically charged as the air was, he might have just whispered her name.

Then he pressed harder, and she knew she'd been righteously kissed. As his tongue swept in, she shot her arms up around his neck and pressed herself close to him.

He broke the kiss enough to speak. "You've given me your needles."

"Hmmm?"

"I've got pins and needles all over my body."

"Are you complaining?"

His answer was a sound deep in his throat as he deepened the kiss.

"Mommy? Can I come on the ladder?"

Annie jumped back a foot. "Savannah, no, honey. I'm coming down. Right now. You wait there."

"We're hungry," Tess called. "Let's go get some lunch."

"I'm on my way. Mr. Cabrini was showing me

how he pulled the plywood off the storage area." She put the flashlight and gloves back in her pockets and returned to the opening.

"Say, Tess," Jack called, "do you want to come up and see a pile of rubbish?"

"You make it sound tempting, but no thanks."

"Move back, sweetheart," Annie said. "I don't want to step on your head." She took the first step down on the ladder, looked up, and was surprised by a quick kiss.

She felt her way down the ladder and skipped the last two rungs to jump to the floor. "So, little girl, you're hungry?"

"A little bit."

She swung Savannah up to her shoulder and hugged her tight. Rather than stare at Jack's very nice-looking buns in tight jeans, she faced the window to the front of the mansion.

"Let's go eat at our house," she said. "I'm going back to the attic this afternoon."

"I'll see the three of you at five, then," Jack asked.

"Umm, Mr. Cabrini has invited us to go swimming at the Rocking Star with Marcy and stay for dinner. I said we're awfully busy, and Savannah doesn't like to swim—"

"Mommy! I do like to swim!" A look of stupefied horror.

"Well," Annie said thoughtfully, "if you say so, I guess we can go."

Savannah hugged Annie's neck tight, so happy she almost floated out of her mother's arms.

"Mommy?" She whispered the question in her ear.

Annie laughed. "Okay, I'll ask. Mr. Cabrini, how old is your sister?"

"Marcy is thirteen. She'll be fourteen in August."

Savannah grinned and whispered again.

"You ask him," Annie said. "I'm not your

personal translator."

Savannah thought about it for a moment, then directed her gaze to Jack. "Can she do a cartwheel?" she asked in a barely audible voice.

"Marcy can do a great cartwheel. And, by the way, I didn't have a chance to tell you yet. She loves your cookies, and she hopes you'll give her the recipe."

To Annie she said, "Can I?"

"Sure. I'll write it down."

She wiggled her legs and hopped down to the floor. "I'll go get my swimsuit!" In a flash she was out the door and on the stairs.

"Thank you." Annie and Tess said it at the same time.

"I'll see you at five. I'd better get back to work."

They watched him leave, and Tess chuckled.

"Well, well, well. Someone isn't so sad anymore."

"Oh, Savannah—" Annie blurted.

"I wasn't referring to Savannah. And you know it."

"I have nothing to say."

"Your face is saying plenty." She threw her arms around Annie. "Let's go rustle up some grub."

"Grub? Are you turning into a cowgirl?"

"Hell, yes. Have you seen the cowboys in this town?"

Chapter Four

Susan Hightower, Deputy United States Marshal, looked up from the copies of Sheldon Roth's letters and official prison records. She'd moved from her cubicle to the conference room for two good reasons. She could read the stuff twice as fast without phones and office chatter. And she coveted the view to the west of Lake Washington and the "back side" of the Seattle skyline, and far beyond that the snowy peaks of the Olympic Mountains.

Under ordinary circumstances, the view soothed her nerves.

But not today.

Today she was pissed.

Here it was Tuesday afternoon. This morning at seven, two hundred twenty-five miles away in Sheridan, Oregon, a white-collar scumbag named Sheldon Roth—alias, alias, alias—walked out of federal prison.

She should have been there. Instead, the FBI was in charge of escorting him to Seattle. Not only were they using kid gloves, they were staying at a distance, content to observe their deal playing out. A photo of Sheldon, snapped with a junior agent's cell phone, made the rounds of computers in her department.

It was offered, said her boss, in a spirit of cooperation.

It was offered, she'd retorted, in the spirit of male dogs peeing where another dog has peed.

She had a lot invested in the case. Luckily, no money. Everyone who invested with Sheldon, by whatever name he'd used, lost their nests as well as their nest eggs.

He was supposed to be locked up for thirty years. Three sentences of approximately ten years, to run consecutively. But a funny thing happened on the way to the hoosegow. The sentencing judge, Walter Sommers, made the three sentences concurrent. Ten years total. "No chance of parole."

Technically, that was observed. Because now, five years and seven months later, he was out—and it wasn't *parole.*

The son of a bitch would be free to leave the country as soon as the FBI, and probably Judge Sommers, got their part of the deal. Money. Not that anyone would admit it.

She clicked again at the icon on the bottom of her computer screen. The cell phone photo of Sheldon Roth appeared. He looked as cocky as he always had, and now he was full through the shoulders and chest. Mr. Muscle. He'd been a workout fanatic in prison. His expensive suit didn't fit so well now.

Her cell phone rang; she checked caller I.D.

"Yes." No need for formality. It was her partner, Michael Hale.

"You were right," he said. "Sommers retired, effective immediately. My friend the court stenographer said his health is not as good as it used to be."

"Neither is mine. Are Shelly and the Feebs back in Seattle?"

"I don't know. Nobody's going to tell us bupkus. You figure any angles from the letters?"

"It's not anything I can use a highlighter on, but I think we should take a look at wife number three. The one with the kid. She moved to Podunk, Montana, a few months ago."

"Why not wife number four? Prospective wife number four. I thought you'd be all over that."

During Sheldon's media-frenzy trial, a Seattle

woman told the press that she and Sheldon were engaged. Mitzi Lucasi got another round of publicity three years into Sheldon's prison sentence, claiming a government conspiracy was ruining her life. She and Sheldon were trying to get married while he was in prison, but the warden stopped the ceremony at the last minute.

The warden said she never got within a mile of the prison, adding that the whole romance was in the woman's mind.

"I don't see Shelly voluntarily tying an albatross around his neck. He's going into hiding, not into the circus. I think she's a deliberate distraction."

"Okay, I'll buy that. But why do you want to look at Annie Riker?"

"She's the only one he impregnated. Well, make that the only one we've discovered. A man who can hide two hundred million dollars can hide a lot of other things. Anyway, I'm going to go talk to Riker's lawyer. You want to meet at Quizno's for lunch?"

"Nah. I've got a doctor's appointment."

Six months ago Mike's brother died from lung cancer, an event that finally got Mike to quit smoking. In addition to wearing a nicotine patch, he was going the hypnosis route and had joined a support group.

The one thing he couldn't do was get a chest X-ray. He was too afraid of what might show up. The hypnotist was working him toward that procedure.

"Okay, sure. Do what you gotta do, Mike. I might go to the range around three. Shooting always cheers me up. Otherwise, the way I feel today, I might bite someone in the fleshy buttocks. You want to shoot, too?"

"That depends. Who were you planning to bite? I might enjoy that more."

"No names. Big brother is probably listening."

Mike laughed. "Call me."

She closed her phone. She and Mike had a lot in

common. Square pegs in round holes. Since no one was eager to work with either of them, they ended up together. However it had happened, it worked. Mike, age forty-nine, had twenty-six years in law enforcement, eighteen of those with the United States Marshals Service. Susan, age thirty-two, had a law degree from University of Washington, nearly nine years in the Marshals Service, and the tenacity of a wolverine.

And a new boss, an ass kisser, who hated her guts.

She neatly placed all the paperwork in folders, put it in her briefcase, and turned off the lights in the conference room.

She'd call on Delia Phinney, whose law office was in the University district. Then, depending on the time, she'd go to the shooting range.

She had to be back to the office for a staff meeting. The twice-weekly meeting that Mike called Happy Hour. Susan called it what she'd called it ever since C. Edgar Sommers became their boss.

The five o'clock butt kiss.

Chapter Five

Jack showered at his cabin and scrubbed his hands with Lava Soap. Funny how comforting that old smell and stinging abrasion was to him.

At the helm of Great Western, Jackson T. Cabrini had to be all about "presentation." Custom-made sports coats and slacks, top of the line shirts of finest Egyptian cotton, silk ties that looked perfect on camera.

Hand-tooled ostrich skin boots, Coors Beer, Bronco tickets on the fifty-yard line, that is, when he wasn't in one corporate sky box or another.

Armani tuxedo, season tickets to the Colorado Symphony Orchestra, and single malt whiskey.

Eye candy on his arm. Willing to go to his place later, for a nightcap.

He never took any of his dates to his place. His home was Marcy's home. The women, whose names he mixed up, had nothing to do with home and Marcy. There had been at least four Jennifers and three named Madison. They'd shared the gene for pretty. Two or three were certifiably beautiful.

But he felt no chemistry. They were, quite simply, forgettable. If he needed a date to a charity event and Jennifer number two was busy, he called Madison number three.

If his life was a stage play, the script now would read: *Enter stage left, Annie Riker. Bring up stage lights*.

Things were getting interesting.

He chuckled. It would be even better if it read: Enter stage left, Annie Riker, wearing a negligee...or a wet T-shirt...or a skimpy towel.

He put on his khaki swim trunks and leaned closer to the mirror to make sure his shave was close. Maybe he should grow a mustache and a neatly trimmed beard. Women loved that. But what if it grew in wiry or—horrors—gray? No, he'd keep shaving. Women loved smooth skin, too.

He backed up a little and tried to see his chest and arms in the over-the-sink mirror. He was fit and tan from running, but his six pack would never make the final callback for a sexy men calendar. Not that he wanted to be on a calendar, but he'd rather *say* "No" than *hear* "No, thanks."

He sighed. *The man in the mirror.* That old chestnut.

The last year or so it wasn't the man in the mirror giving him the *Who do you think you are?* look. It was the men—and women—on the job sites. They'd listen politely and then turn to the supervisor to find out what was actually required. As if CEO Jack Cabrini, in his ultra-shiny hard hat, was there only for a photo op.

As if he didn't know his ass from his elbow. As if the only shovel he knew how to use was the brass shovel with the gold bow slapped into his hands for the ceremonial groundbreaking at his latest project.

Another sigh. He hung up his towel and put away his shaving kit and other toiletries.

Money, even a bucket of money, didn't make up to Jack for that loss of identity. He was a builder. A construction guy. Steel-toed boots. Yes, he had a degree in architecture, but that just made him a better construction guy. He was the son of Ace Cabrini. He had sawdust in his blood.

So, that had been eating at him. But the worst of it was that while he was having his mid-life crisis—or whatever it was—he wasn't doing due diligence for his little sister.

He didn't see that Marcy didn't have real friends, that she was miserable at the expensive private school he sent her to. If he'd tuned in to her frequency, listened to what she was really saying, he could have headed off the trouble.

Instead he'd been a total bonehead. Oblivious. She's got a headache? Take some aspirin. Stomachache? Take some Pepto Bismol. Locked in her room crying? Take—whatever girls take for that.

The only thing he'd been good at was rolling his eyes. Did he think he was living in a sitcom?

"My turn!" Marcy called as she rapped her knuckles on the bathroom door.

He opened the door. She'd already shed her boots and jeans and was trying to untie a knot in her neckerchief. He untied it for her. "Did you have fun on the trail ride?"

"Yeah. Way better than yesterday. No little kids today. We rode all the way to Sweet Spring."

"You smell like a horse."

"Well, *Duh.* You smell like—what is that odor?"

"It's not an odor. It's a men's fragrance. Hurry. They'll be here in fifteen minutes."

She tossed the neckerchief on the pile of dirty clothes and grabbed the swimsuit and cover-up she'd set out on the bed. Racing into the bathroom, she closed the door. A minute later he heard the shower come on.

Uh-oh. Had he left her any hot water?

A sound like a tiger's roar came through the door.

Apparently the answer to his question was *no.*

He had enough time before the Rikers arrived to talk to Travis. Two clicks on his speed dial and he had him.

"McGarry here. Whassup?"

Travis had called Jack at ten a.m. to say he'd gotten an appointment with the D.A.'s chief assistant. The appointment was at three-thirty. Jack had expected to hear from him by now.

"I met with Katerina Woods, the deputy district

attorney. She agreed, grudgingly, to give me ten minutes, but we ended up talking for an hour and five minutes. In fact, after the first ten minutes she said, 'Follow me,' and we marched through a side door to the D.A.'s private office."

Jack clenched his teeth. It could be good news, or it could be totally the opposite. His goal was to make the case go away, to keep Marcy out of the public eye.

On network news, magazines, and internet news, he'd followed four cases of bullying of teenaged girls and three cases where boys were the target. The most famous was the suicide, in Missouri, of a girl Marcy's age. The mother who'd used a fake identity as a teenage boy to taunt the girl online had gotten away with it in Missouri, but a federal grand jury in Los Angeles indicted her. The verdict came in as guilty on three misdemeanor offenses; not guilty of a felony.

In five other cases, the civil suits by outraged parents were shaking up the school boards who'd ignored bullying as it escalated into serious assault. A case involving girls throwing acid in the face of a developmentally disabled teenaged girl was being heard now.

Whatever happened to sugar and spice and everything nice?

"What I didn't know when I walked into the D.A.'s office," Travis said, "was that Crystal DeBeers was charged today in another bullying case, and this time the blowback is huge."

"I'm listening."

"Crystal and her gang have been using school computers to destroy the reputation of Geraldo Domingo."

"Yeah? Go on." Jack tried, but he couldn't place the name.

"Geraldo is the son of the former United States Secretary of the Interior. Valdez Domingo. And did I mention she used *school* computers? Computers at the same school that suspended Marcy for 'lying' about Crystal DeBeers and Heather Janson in the shoplifting case?"

Jack swore. "I'd like to see the look on Vince Safire's face right about now."

"So would I. I wonder if he's going to call me?"

"Bottom line, what's all this going to mean for Marcy?"

"I can't predict that yet, Jack. But I know where you stand. And everybody involved has my number. I'll call you ASAP. If Marcy gets dragged into this, we're going to file a civil suit for every dollar the DeBeers family has. I will make them remove the paint from their walls and present it to you on gold filigree."

Jack sighed. "Call me." He pressed End and set the phone on the small desk. With one knuckle he rapped on the bathroom door.

"Hey, you."

"Hay is for horses."

"Well, well, aren't you the equestrian expert now that you've logged two-point-five hours in the saddle? Hurry up. Our guests are due to arrive."

She opened the door, wearing a one-piece swimsuit and a fishnet cover-up she'd bought on their Christmas trip to Hawaii. "I have to put on lipstick to cover my blue lips, frozen by the cold water you left for me."

"I'm sorry. I'm used to two water heaters."

And a towel heater. And a walk-in shower with piped music in his master suite. And a whirlpool tub.

He held out his hands, palms up. "I guess this is how the pioneers lived."

She applied pink lipstick, slipped her feet in flip-flops, and followed him out the door. "When am I going to see the mansion you're working on?"

"How about tomorrow? I'll ask Annie if she has time to show you around." He knew he wouldn't have time. Getting away early today hadn't been easy. Tomorrow would be a bear.

He was walking a fine line, with the eyes of all the guys, and six women—two of them journeymen electricians—on him. As the new boss, he had to prove himself.

It was an even tougher sell than when he'd come home from college and worked. The boss's son. At least when he took over the whole company after his dad's death, nobody sniped. Or, if they did, no slurs got back to him.

Now he had a new mountain to climb, taking the place of Duke Hemmer, a boss the crew apparently worshiped.

The look of dismay he'd seen on the faces of Annie and Tess Riker had been repeated about thirty times since he'd stepped out of his truck on Albion Hill.

Leaving at four o'clock today could show he was soft, even lazy. Or it could show he trusted his assistant, Gavin LaRue, to do what he was paid and trained to do. Jack hoped it would be taken as confidence in Gavin.

"Here they come," he said to Marcy as the two of them crossed the lawn toward the parking lot. He didn't even try to hide the pleasure he felt to see Annie again. "I think you're going to like them."

****

It was love at first sight.

Annie sipped her margarita through a cocktail straw and watched Savannah walk to the end of the low diving board, fill her whole chest cavity with air, and clamp her fingers over her nostrils. In the water, calling encouragement, was Jack's sister, Marcy.

"One, two, three. Jump."

There was time for a mid-air shriek of delight and giddy fear before Savannah crashed through the surface. As always, Annie flinched and fought the urge to rush to the edge of the pool.

No, no. Stay in my seat.

There, Savannah was chin up and swimming toward the side.

Annie released the breath she'd been holding and took another sip. Maybe "love at first sight" wasn't the correct description. It was more like a baby duck imprinting on the first creature to waddle by after she hatched. Savannah's level of excitement as they drove to Rocking Star Ranch could have fueled a flotilla of hot air balloons. Annie could see that her repeated warnings that maybe Marcy wouldn't be quite as wonderful as Savannah expected fell on deaf ears.

At their introduction by Jack Cabrini, the first words out of Savannah's mouth were, "Can you really do a cartwheel?"

Marcy dropped her towel on the grass and did two cartwheels and a round off. Savannah, wide-eyed with wonder, slapped her hands against her chest as if to hold her heart inside it.

World religions have been established on less devotion than Savannah offered at Marcy's display.

Tess called, "Great job," to Marcy. Then she dropped behind to get a bag she'd left in their car.

Savannah and Marcy sprinted ahead to the pool, and Annie was left to walk alongside Jack. He explained how they were staying at the dude ranch for a week, until their furniture was delivered from Denver.

While he went to the bar to get drinks for the two of them, Annie plunged in and swam the length of the pool and back. It was sheer delight. And thanks to her new hairdo, all she had to do was shake her head and run her fingers through it.

It was heavenly to stretch out on the chaise lounge and let the sun warm her up.

Now she glanced at Jack as she sipped her drink. Instead of joining Tess and Tree Autrey, owner of the dude ranch, at a nearby table, he'd chosen to sit on the grass beside her chaise lounge. On one hand, she was pleased, but at the same time she was wary of too much "friendship" in what was a business relationship. She could tell herself—and did tell herself, repeatedly—that socializing like this was no different than businessmen playing golf and drinking beer together, but...it was way different. Insanely different.

They'd already kissed.

Getting better acquainted, as they officially were, took on a whole other meaning after what had happened in the attic. She was tingling all over in a most unbusinesslike way. And she hadn't missed the appreciative look on Jack's face as he languidly surveyed her ninety percent naked body.

She should have worn a one-piece suit. Hell, she should have worn a bathing costume from 1890. The bloomers and short sleeves would have covered her flush of embarrassment.

Embarrassment? Ha. Rush of excitement was more like the truth. Jack Cabrini had what her friends called "bedroom eyes." She was going to have to stay cool around him. Cool, reserved. Businesslike. But the air temperature was about eighty—and summer wasn't even here yet.

"I can't believe what I'm seeing," she said to Jack as her little girl went off the board for the third time. "Savannah knows how to swim, but she's never jumped off a diving board before. She'll do anything to impress Marcy. She's like Dumbo with the magic feather."

"It's good for Marcy to be adored for once. Being thirteen, almost fourteen, is ninety percent angst. And moving here, where she doesn't know anyone, makes it even harder."

"But you did move," she said. "By choice."

He sighed and rubbed his forehead. "Temporary increase in angst in exchange for long-term improvement. Denver wasn't...I mean, she'll be better off in a small town. And better off with me working normal hours."

"Running such a huge company must have been demanding."

He said nothing, but again she saw that shadow of worry she'd seen at Albion House. It was in his face and his shoulders, and it seemed to show up every time he mentioned Denver.

"Do you have any other family who helped you out? In Seattle I always had Tess and my dad, so when I got stuck on the wrong side of a bridge shutdown, or stopped behind a ten-car pileup, I could send an S.O.S." She thought about it. "I guess it was actually a P.U.S. Pick Up Savannah, before the daycare center closes."

"No—when my dad and stepmother died in a plane crash, Marcy and I were left with no family but each other. And I'd been living in Europe. I'd never even seen her."

"And she was how old?"

"Two. But we do have Vera Stefano, my father's administrative secretary for many years, and then mine. She acts *in loco parentis* for both Marcy and me. She moved here with us, to her own place. It was the only way I could get her to retire."

They watched the girls join a haphazard game of keep away in the shallow end. Jack rose and stretched. Reaching over his head, he pulled his shirt off and dropped it beside her lounge chair.

"If I don't go into the pool, Marcy will hound me without mercy. Care to join me?"

"Thanks, no. I just got dry. I'll watch."

She smiled as he arched off the diving board with athletic grace. Watching Jack Cabrini, she admitted to herself, was nice work if you could get it. He wore khaki trunks slung low on his hips; his tanned and muscled chest and arms, and his narrow waist, showed to excellent advantage. She was grateful that he hadn't worn a tiny swatch of cloth that displayed the shape of a man's equipment with the same lack of subtlety as the covers of bodybuilder magazines. Not her style, not at all.

Annie watched him surface beside Marcy, who shrieked her surprise and clambered up on his shoulders. Savannah looked around and waved when she saw her mom.

Annie laughed and thanked heaven that Marcy was still on the girl side of the girl-woman divide. Several of her friends in Seattle had teenage daughters, and Annie had heard quite a few tales of sweet, loving little girls who'd morphed into surly strangers.

She'd seen the ugly transformation firsthand with the daughter of her friend Elle, a museum curator. The four of them, Elle and Emma, Annie and Savannah, got together about twice a month for three years. And then...not so much. Emma turned into a sour, scowling, angry girl who used foul language, even around Savannah. To impress the popular girls in her school, Emma had taken Elle's credit card and bought clothes fit for a streetwalker.

Annie had ended the foursomes the first time Emma had cursed at her mother in front of Savannah. She'd tried to maintain her friendship with Elle as occasional lunch dates, but all Elle could talk about was the trouble Emma was getting into. Meanwhile, Elle, who'd lost seventy pounds and kept it off for five years, was piling it back on. That, too, became her topic.

As much as anything else about the Elle and Emma soap opera, Annie was alarmed by the fact that Emma had no father. Elle had been open—too open, in Annie's opinion—in saying she'd used a sperm bank to get pregnant. She'd thought such honesty would keep her daughter close to her. Elle's model was a loving "you and me against the world" alliance; but Emma used "sperm donor" to slice and dice her mother. It was Elle's fault she'd been suspended from school for three days, or kicked off the school bus, or whatever the current issue was. No trouble Emma got into was her fault, according to Emma. And Elle bought into the blame-a-thon. Emma's rough patch—an absurd euphemism in Annie's opinion—was all because she didn't have a father.

Annie shuddered every time she thought of Savannah throwing that in her face some day. She wished for an insurance policy that would guarantee a well-loved child would grow up to be loving, but no such policy was on the market. At the end of the day, or at the end of approximately twelve years, every parent threw the dice.

Jack swam to the edge of the pool and hauled himself out. She tossed him his towel, and he sat beside her. They soaked up the sunshine in companionable silence.

She noticed he rotated his neck as if it were stiff. Without thinking, she stretched out her hand and massaged it.

"Thanks," he said. "I've been using muscles that must have gone dormant. I considered rubbing on some Ben-Gay, but then I thought, maybe not on our first date."

She laughed softly and rubbed more vigorously. First date? Why did that sound so special? Because, she conceded to herself, it implied more to come. Like licking the spoon while the brownies baked in the oven. *More to come.*

The clang of the dinner bell outside the dining hall got the kids out of the pool. Marcy and Tess followed the chattering girls to Jack and Marcy's cabin to change into jeans and western shirts.

When they met Jack in the buffet line, he was explaining to Tree Autrey how Vera Stefano needed hip replacement surgery.

"I invited her to come tonight," he added, "but

she's not up to it. We expect to get the surgery date tomorrow."

"You let me know if there's anything we can do to help," Tree said. "She's a keeper."

He was referring to Vera, but Annie noticed he looked at Tess when he said it.

Tree and Tess had met two months earlier at a county council hearing about use of the one-quarter percent Lodgers Tax to increase tourism, but they kept finding reasons to meet for coffee, and Annie was pretty sure it wasn't caffeine dependence. Tree was tall, thin, and as true-west as the quarter horses on his dude ranch. Never married, he was in his early or maybe mid-forties.

"Tree has some good ideas for joint advertising in airline magazines," Tess said a week ago as she'd hurried to meet him at the Roundup Cafe.

Annie had barked a laugh. "I think Tree has some other ideas, too. No, wait. You said he's 'just a friend.'"

"There's nothing wrong with cordiality in a business relationship," Tess said with a haughty toss of her hair.

"Cordiality?" Annie had hooted. "Is that what you call it?"

Now she wasn't hooting; she wasn't even snickering. She and the general contractor of the Albion House project had explored levels of cordiality she could barely believe existed.

After dinner she and Savannah joined Jack and Marcy to tour the horse barn. Marcy named all the horses and described their idiosyncrasies, with Savannah hanging on every word as holy.

Gradually, the girls drifted off, invited to another girl's cabin, and Annie was left with Jack. They wandered aimlessly, in the general direction of the duck pond, finally sitting on a wrought iron bench.

A male and female mallard wandered out of the

pond and edged close to the bench.

"Somebody expects handouts," Jack said. "Sorry, nothing tonight, folks."

A pair of swans drifted gracefully toward the shore.

"What kind of swans do you think those are?" Annie asked.

"Tundra swans. I only know it because I heard Tree Autrey tell somebody else. Trumpeter swans look a lot like Tundras, but they're bigger."

"I like swans," she said softly. "I like that they mate for life."

Jack said nothing; she regretted sounding like such a hopeless romantic.

At last he sighed. "That's my ideal, too. But I guess I take it even further—at least I did for my dad."

She waited. He seemed to be wrestling with something he wanted to say.

"He loved my mom as long as she lived. But he had better sense than the kind of birds that never take another mate. He fell in love again. But I—I couldn't accept it. Instead, I acted like a horse's ass and never did a thing to heal the wound."

"Are you talking about your dad, or mine?" she asked.

"Definitely my father. I don't know your dad."

"He's a man," she said.

"Ummm, you say that like it's a bad thing."

"I have my reasons." She shrugged. "Sorry. Sometimes I let my anger at the man I married spill over. I guess 'reason' is the wrong word in this case."

He put his arm around her shoulders and gave a gentle squeeze. "Okay, new subject. Your choice."

"I appreciate your magnanimity, but I have to stick with the subject of my marital misadventure."

"I'm a good listener."

She watched the swans while she collected her thoughts.

"I've been a sensible person ninety-five percent of my life. If I were a shoe, I wouldn't be a red sling-back. I'd be a tan athletic shoe. A cross trainer. Bought on sale. But my good sense was no match for Peter Dylan."

She paused. Jack squeezed her hand. *Go on.*

"I met him when I was hired to design display space in a new museum for an exhibit of Victoriana."

"What's that?"

"Art, clothing, literature, dishes—everything that showed how people with money lived in the age of Queen Victoria."

"And he was interested in that?"

"He appeared to be. Everything about Peter was an appearance. He was like a perfect silver fish seen through the surface of a clear lake. He was never where or what he seemed. He seemed to be unspeakably wealthy. Turned out he was just unspeakable."

She withdrew her hand from Jack's and wiped the sweat on her jeans.

"While he was riding high, he pursued me with extravagant flowers and really thoughtful, quirky, funny surprises. I got swept up in how romantic he was. It was like...ummm, it was like a script for a romantic comedy. And it didn't hurt that he looked like Hugh Jackman." She sighed. "Skipping over the part where I fell in love, which nauseates me to recall, I went with him to Hawaii. We got married on the beach on Kauai."

Jack took her right hand again and threaded their fingers in and out. "Go on."

"When we got back to Seattle, we kept our marriage a secret. My dad and Tess knew, but Peter had a son from a former marriage, and he wanted to break it to him first. He said his son was nineteen and troubled. 'Probably bipolar,' he said. If his son read about us in the paper, it could send him into a downward spiral. I was fine with waiting. But I knew six weeks after the wedding that I was pregnant, which made me ecstatically happy."

"Where did his son live?"

She barked a short laugh. "There wasn't any son. And there wasn't any ex-wife. There were, however, two current wives. Married to him under two of his aliases."

Jack whistled. "When did you find that out?"

"After he was arrested. I was three months along in the pregnancy. Of course I thought the arrest was all a horrible mistake. But, trust me, it was no mistake. He'd built a financial house of cards, and when it crashed, it crashed big. You probably heard about it."

"What was his name? Not Peter Dylan, I gather."

"Sheldon Roth."

"Oh, boy. Roth."

"Made the news, yeah. He made a lot of money disappear. A lot of people were hurt, and some charitable foundations. Ugly, ugly."

"You were dragged in, I'm sure."

"I got an attorney, Delia Phinney. She went with me, and my dad and Tess, to the United States Attorney's office. It was a good thing I did, too, because they knew all about me. And I do mean *all* about me. Wiretaps. Photo surveillance."

She cleared her throat. "At first they couldn't believe anyone was as stupid as I claimed to be. 'No, really, it's true,' I remember saying. 'I'm a moron.'"

She shrugged. "Pretty sad, isn't it, when my best defense is limited mental capacity? Gradually, they came to believe it. I, however, still can't believe it."

"So nothing bad happened to you? I mean, legally. Obviously, plenty of bad happened."

"Right. I was collateral damage. Roadkill. Not involved in any of Sheldon's schemes." She wrung her hands, squeezing them hard, as if the more pain she felt, the better it would be. "The money he'd wasted on me for flowers and our trip to Hawaii was negligible against the backdrop of massive fraud. I didn't even have a diamond ring."

She held her bare left hand out, rigid, and stared at it. The shame of being so dumb stabbed at her.

"Lucky for me," she said with a snort of derision, "there's no such felony as First Degree Gullible."

Annie glanced sideways at Jack. A muscle along his clenched jaw line twitched. She was pretty sure whatever passed for romance between the two of them had been pinched out like a candle flame.

"Let's walk," Jack said.

Six years ago, she'd been forced by circumstances to tell her story again and again, but it hadn't gotten easier. The same way five and a half years of motherhood had made her forget the pain of childbirth, time had washed out the pain of telling dozens of strangers how she'd married Peter Dylan. But now, telling Jack Cabrini, the shame burned again.

Side by side they strolled slowly around the duck pond, moving apart twice for kids on in-line skates.

She sucked in a deep breath. The sooner she got this over with, the sooner she could collect Savannah, go home, and get back to a purely business relationship with Jack.

"So, I learned that he had at least three aliases and that he'd defrauded investors. For the first two days after his arrest, I lived in absolute terror of seeing my face on TV. Turned out to be good news— bad news. When they put photos of Sheldon Roth's wife up, it was a woman in New York City. Then the other woman turned up. She lived in Portland, Oregon, and was married to Peter Roth. Since they only needed two wives to hang a bigamy charge on, the feds didn't run me up the flagpole." She paused. "Actually, that's not totally true. They wanted me to testify against him, but I wouldn't. The stress was very bad, and my doctor said I could lose the baby if they didn't leave me alone."

"Roth knew you were pregnant?"

She nodded and walked faster. "I told him the minute I found out. By phone. Which means I was sharing my joy with God-only-knows-how-many federal agents."

"Wasn't he sentenced to something like thirty years?"

"Sort of. That's what the judge said publicly, but instead of three sentences to run consecutively, he set them to run concurrently. Roughly, ten years. But all that has changed." She looked at her watch. "This morning I received a registered, special delivery letter from his attorney. Sheldon Roth is out of prison, free—no parole. He's even getting his passport back, and he plans to leave the country and stay far away."

"You're saying he's about to be gone, presumably forever. Why do I sense a second shoe is about to fall?"

"More like a boot." Again she increased her speed. By now it barely qualified as a walk. "He knows I want him to relinquish any claim of paternity. Sign away any rights. My lawyer has sent the document to him three times, but he refused to sign it."

"You don't think he wants anything to do with Savannah, do you?"

"No. The letter I got this morning says he wants to see her one time. Then he will sign the document. And he's planning to leave the country with no intention to ever return."

"You believe that?"

"Actually, I do. My lawyer thinks he turned in someone the feds really wanted, maybe a federal judge, but that's just a guess. Maybe he found someone inside the prison and court system who's as crooked as he is, and he simply bought his way out. Nobody, and I mean nobody doubts that he has money stashed somewhere—enough to buy his way out and still live like a king. But this is the thing. He has a lot of enemies. To protect his own life, he'll disappear."

They were back at the bench. She sat on it, glad to get off her legs, which felt like rubber.

"Somebody could probably write a bestseller based on how he got out," she concluded.

"Are you going along with his request?" He sat beside her.

"I'll do almost anything to get him out of Savannah's life forever."

And out of mine.

"Where? When?" He took her hand in his and gently kneaded it.

The minute he touched her, she knew she'd been deluding herself to think the romance was all gone. Did he feel the current of electricity she felt? Of course, the only other time she'd felt that power surge had led to disaster. Her judgment about men was notoriously bad. One man, one shipwreck.

"Savannah and I will go to Seattle. Delia is setting it up. I know it has to be soon." She looked down at their hands and thought, as she had beside the pool, how *comfortable* she felt with him. Yes, she found him sexy and exciting, but beneath that extravagantly fancy frosting was good old-fashioned chocolate cake. Comfort food.

The kind of man who liked snow sports followed by mulled wine. Beside a fireplace—and a stack of good books.

Somebody could write a bestseller about that, too!

Cherry Adair, please call your agent.

She looked into his eyes. To keep from kissing him, she stood, abruptly. To keep from putting her arms around his neck, she shoved her hands into her front pockets.

Jack stood, too. "Let's go see what our girls are up to."

"Yes. I was about to say that."

On the way, she cleared her throat. "I'm surprised that you chose Bitter Falls. I hope Marcy won't be disappointed by small-town life. She must have had a lot going on in Denver."

"I'm pretty sure Bitter Falls will suit both of us. But, hey—you have the same transition. Seattle is a world away from this place."

"This is better for Savannah," Annie said without hesitation.

"There, you see?" He smiled. "We're both looking for a good family place."

"Another subject, then," she said. "If you're selling Great Western, what will your new smaller company be called?"

"I'm working on that. Suggestions are welcome. I'm running through the obvious: Bitter, River, Mountain, Falls. Each of those followed by View. Not working for me."

"Why not your last name? The C in Cabrini goes with Construction."

"I like alliteration as much as the next guy, and I want to be close to the start of the alphabet to get the phone book advantage, but I don't want my name on it."

"How about Acme?"

"Like in the Roadrunner cartoons? Mail order disaster kits? Not so much the thought I want to plant in the mind of customers. But that gives me an idea."

He paused, seemed to weigh the idea. "Yeah, I've got it. Ace Construction. My dad's name was Alphonse. He went by Ace from the time he was old enough to carry a shoeshine kit. I don't know why I didn't think of it before this."

Almost two hours later, Annie's plans to get

Savannah home for an early bedtime were OBE, a phrase Jack liked to use. Overtaken By Events. It was an expression he said applied in many situations, political, business, and personal. Annie's statement that she and Savannah probably ought to be leaving was ignored—at least three times—by everyone as a quartet of singing and guitar-playing cowboys assembled on the patio and led the guests in old favorites.

"Home on the Range," "There's a Long, Long Trail A-winding," "Red River Valley," and "You Are My Sunshine."

Annie watched the magical look of joy on Savannah's face. Although she didn't know the words to most of the songs, she was clearly in a state of rapture. When the quartet sang, "This Land is Your Land," they called up Marcy and Savannah to help them with the chorus. Annie wished she had a camera. Instead she seared the image on her memory.

At last they sang the last song, "Happy Trails to You," and guests drifted away in the moonlight. Tree Autrey offered Tess a ride, and she accepted. Marcy went to their cabin while Jack walked Annie and Savannah to their car.

As Savannah fastened her seatbelt, her eyes fluttered sleepily. Annie looked at Jack, and at the almost full moon over his head.

"Thanks for a lovely evening," she said. "I guess I'll see you tomorrow?"

A kiss would be welcome, she thought, but so, so wrong. So inappropriate. So—

"Good night," he said, brushing his lips like feathers on her cheek.

Only the presence of Savannah in the backseat kept her from grabbing him by the shoulders and giving him a full frontal embrace. Instead she whispered, "Good night."

As she drove to their small rented home, she

sang softly the last lines of the song. "Happy trails to you, until we meet again."

Chapter Six

Jack was up before dawn on Wednesday. Naturally a morning person, his happiest memories of his two years in Italy were not of the food, or the wine, or the women, but of the sun coming up in Tuscany.

Over the Colosseum in Rome was great, too. And over the Adriatic Sea.

Sunrise in the Montana mountains was just as beautiful, though completely different. Each day was fresh and full of opportunity. And meeting Annie Riker—*kissing Annie Riker!*—was an explosion of opportunity. Even his toenails were involved in the celebration that thrummed in his bloodstream.

Annie, Annie, Annie.

He stopped to catch his breath but kept moving his legs so the muscles wouldn't cramp. He'd signed up, before he left Denver, for membership at the small Better Bods gym in a storefront on Maple Street. Memo to self: visit the weight room before this week is over.

He finished the six-mile run and walked a quarter mile or so around the ranch's outbuildings to cool down. A thin film of mist floated above the creek that crossed the pasture, flowing into more substantial fog that marked the Bitter River to the east.

Up a gentle slope, maybe three miles as the eagle flies, was the rim of the Rocking Star's land. At that point the paved highway that seemed headed toward the ranch angled away toward a scenic canyon. In the clear morning air, he could hear the sound of an eighteen wheeler shifting down for the climb.

That one noise brought Denver back. He'd lived there so long he'd stopped noticing the constant traffic noise. Perpetual pounding of wheels on freeways. Vibration day and night that people grew to accept as normal.

Only when sirens came within a block did Jack even glance in their direction. And the brown soup of pollution had become another normal. Every time he left the mountains to return to the geological bowl of the metro area, he saw the soup from above and dreaded to descend.

Montana offered a fresh start to his lungs, his mind, his sister. And, if kissing Annie Riker was everything he believed it to be, a fresh start to his heart.

He strolled across the spacious patio, where last night he'd sat on a stump close by Annie's chair. When they all sang the words, "Come and sit by my side if you love me," he'd taken her hand in his.

He laughed and shook his head. Annie Riker had no way of knowing, but for Jackson T. Cabrini, that simple gesture was ultra romantic. He hadn't stayed single until age thirty-nine and a half by accident.

Before heading to the cabin to shower, he stopped by the kitchen of the lodge and poured a mug of coffee from the gigantic urn, then slipped back out the side door.

Perched on the edge of the porch, he listened to the soft morning sounds of horses nickering and the farm report on the kitchen radio.

"Good morning." Two wranglers returned his greeting as they walked horses to the barn for breakfast and bridles. Marcy was going on the nine a.m. ride; he'd better wake her up.

Tess Riker was picking her up at one o'clock and taking her to Albion House for a tour. He chuckled, thinking how Savannah would shadow Marcy's every move.

It was going to be a good day.

****

"Mommy, when can we get a puppy?"

Since the moment her eyes snapped open, Savannah had talked about Marcy, and horses, and swimming, and tumbling lessons, and puppies. Words burbled out of her like water from a mountain spring. Annie glanced at her in the rearview mirror.

"We'll have to talk about a puppy later. Mrs. Hamilton is waiting for me, to talk about the upholstery."

She pulled into the dirt lot along two sides of the prefab metal building. The front two thirds was a custom glass and tile store; the back third was an upholstery shop. A smaller prefab, also in that lot, was the storage building she and Tess were renting to store their finished and unfinished furniture and other fixtures, such as bathroom sinks. Only two of the sinks had arrived; another shipment from a custom plumbing company in Billings would arrive by truck in ten days.

Savannah knew the rules at the "pose-tree" shop. She could play with the books of samples as long as she put them back in the same order on Mrs. Hamilton's shelf.

Annie and Jo-Jo Hamilton went over the wallpaper samples that had come in from San Francisco. They didn't want to risk touching scissors to cloth for chairs and loveseats until they had firm commitments of delivery on the wallpaper.

"The old rose and the sage green are perfect," Annie said, "but will they ever give us a firm delivery date?"

She showed Jo-Jo digital pictures of the armoires and library tables. "As for delivery," she said, "the antique dealer in Missoula was vague about the date. I'm going to call him today."

"Well, just let me know roughly when you expect

the truck and one of us, me or George, will be here to take delivery."

"Thanks. I appreciate that." Her cell phone rang, and she looked at the caller ID. It was her lawyer in Seattle.

"Jo-Jo, would it be all right if Savannah played here a few minutes? I need to take this call."

"Sure, you go ahead."

"Hello?" She moved quickly to an old couch behind the display area.

"Hi, Annie. How are you holding up?"

"Umm, compared to what? I think my body temperature was about ninety degrees after I read the letter. It's normal now. Oh, and I only threw up twice."

She didn't mention that her body temperature and pulse rate had soared, yesterday in the attic, when a certain construction guy took her in his arms. Nor did she mention it happened again last night at the guest ranch.

"This is going to be rough for you," Delia said. "Of that I have no doubt. But it will be over soon. The scumbag will be gone."

"Where do you think he'll go? I only care to know because I want it to be far away. Outer Mongolia. The top of Mount Everest. Deep under water would be good, too."

"Nobody's giving out that information. From what little I've squeezed out of a friend in the U.S. Attorney's office, I think Sheldon Roth will be dropping as far off the radar as he can. Nobody doubts that he has money he hasn't disclosed. Money hidden so well that in five years of looking the FBI couldn't find it."

"How do you think he got out? I know, it doesn't matter. It's nothing to me. But—I'm curious."

"Even my friend won't tell me, and I introduced her to her current husband, who is making her ridiculously happy. However, my guess is it's connected to the arrest ten days ago of Herbert Magnusson."

"And he is—?"

"Oh, I forget, you live in the backwoods. Magnusson is a federal district court judge. The FBI and the U.S. Attorney have both investigated him so long, with no charges, that everyone forgot about it. But all of a sudden, he's in handcuffs on the front page of the Seattle Times. The indictment is sealed for another six days, which is enough time for Sheldon-the-Chameleon to blow the U.S.A. Coincidence? Maybe. But Sheldon had to come up with something really, really big to get out."

"What about the meeting?" Annie sighed. She'd rather donate a kidney than drag Savannah anywhere near her ex-whatever.

"Friday, ten a.m. I decided the three of us will go to Chenoweth, et cetera, and meet Isaac Chenoweth and Sheldon in their conference room. We'll take a portable DVD player and pop 'Sleeping Beauty' in. Opiate of the little people. Savannah won't even notice there are men in the room. Ten minutes later, you and Savannah leave. I'll stay to get the paper signed and filed with the court. Voila!"

Annie exhaled. "I thought you wanted them to come to your office."

"I had second thoughts. Improved thoughts. It's harder to get people to leave than it is to leave. Also, just in case a hit man is following Sheldon Roth, I don't want to open the door to my office."

Annie shuddered at the thought of some killer standing or hiding anywhere near Savannah. This meeting was going to be so over so fast.

"I'm going to hate every second of this, but I know we have to do it."

"One more thing. Do you remember Susan Hightower?"

"United States Marshal?"

"Deputy, yes. She came to see me yesterday

afternoon. The FBI has taken over Sheldon and won't let the Marshals Service anywhere near him. Since Susan was so heavily involved in bringing him to justice—"

"Is that what you call it?" Annie interrupted. "The so-called thirty-year sentence?"

"Susan is furious, too. She has some theories of what the FBI is up to, but I couldn't wheedle them out of her. In any event, she offered to go to the meeting with us, on Friday. I said yes. Can't hurt to have an armed escort. And it will annoy the hell out of the FBI. I never miss an opportunity to do that."

"Sure. That's fine. Let's get it over with."

"Good thinking. Give Savannah a hug and kiss from me. And don't forget 'Sleeping Beauty.' Disney always works on my girls. Hell, it works on me. I'm still singing 'Someday my prince will come.'"

Annie closed her phone and sagged back against the couch. Delia was cross-referencing her Disney princesses. The one who sang, "Someday my prince will come" was Snow White.

Sleeping Beauty was the princess hidden in a cottage in the woods for sixteen years to avoid contact with a spinning wheel. She was cursed by a witch to die when she pricked her finger, but the curse was mitigated to sleeping for as long as it took for her prince to show up and kiss her.

Right now, the notion of locking Savannah away from the world to keep her safe had a certain appeal.

She laughed as she got back on her feet. Safety was appealing, but she didn't like the rest of that story. Why should some self-proclaimed prince waltz in and claim her daughter with a kiss?

Time to buy a shotgun, before Savannah gets any prettier.

On the way home, Savannah brought up the puppy issue again. She'd acquired potent new ammunition during their visit to the Rocking Star: Marcy was getting a puppy.

And not just "someday," either. Marcy was getting a puppy in two weeks.

"And we can get sister puppies, so they can visit each other just like you said." Savannah was heading for a career as a marketing guru. Or as a high-powered attorney.

Annie wondered what she'd been thinking when she'd made up that malarkey about getting a puppy born in Bitter Falls so it could "visit its family." It had been an expedient excuse at the pet store in Missoula. Now, it was back like a boomerang.

"I don't think Mr. Jamison will let us have a puppy in our little house. When we rented it I said we didn't have a pet."

"But you could ask him," Savannah pointed out in an exasperated tone that said, *Do I have to think of everything?*

"I'll call Mr. Jamison tonight, if I have time. And that's all I'm going to say about it right now. Quit while you're ahead, Savannah."

Two more months in the rented house and the three of them should be able to move into Albion House. Chaos would still reign supreme in seventy percent of the mansion, but the private residence section should be complete.

She sighed and made a note to talk to Jack about that schedule. Along with questions about the puppy issue. If Savannah were to be believed, Jack and Marcy had found a litter of "the best puppies in the world" and were taking their little paragon of perfection home, to their new house, in two weeks.

Her cell phone rang. "Hello?"

"It's me," Tess said. "When will you be home?"

"Two minutes. Why?"

"I'm going to pick up Marcy at one, but Tree invited the three of us to come early and have lunch, too."

"Savannah can go; she'd love it. I'm tied up. See you in a minute." She closed her phone as she turned onto the street with dozens of trees budding and four gorgeous flowering crabapples in full blossom.

Tess stood in the driveway beside her silver Jeep.

Ten minutes later Annie was alone, determined to use the quiet time to start digging through the correspondence sent to her by Goldie's law firm. Good sense told her to stay there, in the silent house, but she didn't want to miss Marcy's reaction to Albion House. And, of course, she would enjoy watching Savannah follow Marcy like a sunflower follows the sun.

And there was one more reason. The chance to see Jack Cabrini was a powerful pull.

"What is happening to me?" she muttered.

The same thing that happened to me six-and-a-fraction years ago.

She'd fallen in love with Peter Dylan, or at least with the man she thought Peter Dylan was, and it felt exactly like this.

Heart pounding. Hands sweaty. Breasts tingling, aching to be caressed. Caught at first like a kite in a freshening breeze, Annie had soared and spun—dizzy with love—in a whirlwind.

Then Peter pulled the earth out from under her.

She'd fallen. And fallen. And fallen. Until she hit granite. Bedrock. And swore: never again.

I should stay away from Jack Cabrini.

Determined to focus on something she could do instead of someone she wished to kiss, she spread the contents of the white box on her bed and arranged it by dates, an easy task thanks to large clips used by someone at the law firm. Her plan was to read the oldest material first, but instead she gathered a sheaf of letters from the 1960s. Her mother was born, and immediately adopted, in 1960. When—and how—had Goldie discovered that she had a granddaughter?

To Annie, Goldie Jones, Stanley, and Greta were

characters in a novel. But her mother was real.

She parked in front and began her ascent of Albion Hill. Jack had told her she could park safely in back, but she had a picture in her mind of a cement truck making a big oops and destroying her baby-blue Ford Escape Hybrid. She'd rather climb.

Fourteen months ago, about three weeks after she and Tess had heard from Dusart and Dusart that they were heirs to a fortune, she'd climbed these stairs in rugged winter boots. What a sad, decrepit old house she'd discovered.

Amelia Holt, granddaughter of Goldie's sister, Violet, still lived there three or four months of the year. At seventy-five, Amelia was athletic and graceful. In addition to biking, swimming and golf, she was a serious devotee of the tango. For some four years, she'd been living about half the year in Arizona, when she wasn't traveling. Her living quarters at Albion House had shrunken to her large bedroom on the second floor and the kitchen on the first floor.

Amelia couldn't be there to meet Annie and Tess, but she'd arranged for an old friend to open up the walled-off solarium and the bedroom wings. Her friend had come to Albion House early that morning and tried to force some heat into "the old girl" with a combination of three fireplaces and a cranky old oil furnace, but the cold was stubborn. Two of the fireplaces refused to draw.

Albion House was like an old woman with a grudge. It was hard to love.

Now Annie lifted the heavy plastic where the custom front door would go and walked inside. And laughed.

Albion House fourteen months ago was the Westin Hotel compared to what it looked like today. With its wallboard ripped out, plaster in piles, and wiring exposed, the mansion was a monstrosity. At this point it was like watching sausage get made. If she hadn't witnessed this process before, the evisceration of an old house before reconstruction could begin, she'd weep instead of laugh.

But even with the advantage of experience and faith in their contractor, she found it extremely difficult to believe they would accept their first B&B guests in three-and-a-half months.

She knew that a tremendous amount of work had already been done. In October, before winter weather set in, the three chimneys were repaired and cleaned and the roof was replaced. At the same time, everything belonging to Amelia Holt was removed. Her granddaughter, Luanne Holt, who lived in Bitter Falls, had arranged for storage.

In November a crew had taken all the remaining furniture, dishes, et cetera to the heated storage building beside the upholstery shop for Annie and Tess to sift through when they had time. On the Monday after Thanksgiving, workers had started ripping out the old kitchen, bathrooms, and some walls.

Annie'd lost count of how many giant dumpsters they'd filled and hauled away.

Which reminded her—she had only two days to poke around in the attic before a crew went up there and dragged everything out for disposal. Jack's plan for the new heating and cooling system, a revolutionary new heat pump system that used solar cells from the Suncatcher factory, needed that space for staging and easy access for maintenance.

She took the stairs to her favorite spot—so far—in Albion House, the window bench on the third-floor landing. Noise from the construction crew in back of the mansion was muted there, and the scenery was spectacular. Annie had no way of knowing, but she believed Goldie Jones had liked this spot.

It was like a widow's watch on a sea captain's house, but without the sea, and sheltered from the wind.

Goldie had refused all her life to have the mansion designated a historic landmark. According to the docents at the local historical museum, Goldie believed—rightly or wrongly—that the government wanted to dictate what she could do with her property.

Her older sister, Violet, died at the age of ninety. Ten years later, Goldie died, age ninety-seven. Both had been widows for many years. How eccentric they must have seemed. And what history they'd witnessed. They'd grown up the daughters of sodbusters in Minnesota. Like *Little House on the Prairie*. And Goldie had braved the Klondike.

After Goldie's death, Violet's son Girard Kellum and later his daughter, Amelia Kellum Holt, had respected Goldie's dictum. No historical society or government entity had any say in how Albion House was or was not remodeled.

Only a week ago, Duke had assured Annie and Tess that the project was past the halfway mark. A lot of work being done elsewhere would slide into place at the right time. Solar panels, high-tech windows, and the beautiful fixtures and appliances they'd selected would arrive on schedule.

Once the flooring was complete, specialized crews would install all the fixtures and appliances. At approximately the same time, other crews would finish out the rooms with paint and wallpaper.

Also, the finishing touches would be done on the wedding gazebo. Set on a slightly higher shoulder of Albion Hill to the west of the mansion, the gazebo would be the central feature of their brochure. Brides would walk out the west door of the solarium and mount the gentle steps.

Their first guests would be travel agents, three or four at a time, at the end of August and the first two weeks of September. Then, the second weekend of September, would be the real stress test of their hospitality. A large wedding party was booked for four days. The wedding would take place in the gazebo and the reception in the solarium. All the market research Tess had done pointed toward wedding events as big moneymakers for scenic inns and bed and breakfasts. A close second was family reunions.

What irony. A mansion built by a woman who drove away her only surviving son and who never laid eyes on her descendants will be known as a perfect place to bring families together.

"Hi. I saw your car out front."

Annie looked up from the painfully faint, hard to read photocopy she was studying.

Damn! Her mouth watered. Literally.

Her eyes popped. Figuratively.

Jack Cabrini looked good enough to lick. Blue jeans soft from many washings, scuffed cowboy boots, and a black cotton T-shirt stretched tight across the muscles of his chest.

What she said was, "Hi." What she thought was, *That cotton died for a good cause.*

"Marcy called," he said. "Said she's having lunch with Tess and Savannah. And Tree Autrey."

"Tess does quite a lot with Tree Autrey."

"You're frowning."

"I am?" She pressed her forehead. "My dad calls me Saran Wrap, says he can see right through me."

"Umm, maybe he can, but I can't. Ann-Marie Riker is a woman of mystery."

She blushed, and a giggle—a giggle!—escaped from her lips.

"Come on, out with it. It's not polite to laugh alone."

She clamped her lips together and shook her head. There was no way she'd tell him she was thinking about a romance novel in which the heroine greeted the hero wearing nothing but Saran Wrap.

"Want to share my lunch?" He held up a paper sack.

She gathered the paperwork she'd spread on the window seat and set it on the floor. "I hate liverwurst."

"So do I. How about turkey and provolone?"

"Perfect. But I don't want to take your food away. You're working hard, whereas I'm just sitting here, sorting through stories about dead people."

"I have plenty of lunch for both of us." He sat beside her, handed her half a sandwich, and nodded toward the plastic bottle at her feet. "I see you have some water."

"Umm-hmm. Thanks." She took a bite and watched his face as he surveyed the scenery.

"The new windows for this landing have arrived." He took another bite, chewed and swallowed. "With the butter-cream paint you selected, this will be a great spot."

She nodded, swallowed. "Oh, at the risk of biting the hand that feeds me, I have a bone to pick with you, Mr. Cabrini."

"A bone? Sounds serious."

"Savannah tells me—over and over—that Marcy is getting a puppy in two weeks. And that there are more puppies in this litter from heaven."

"Are you looking for a pup?"

"Savannah's first word, when she was sixteen months old, wasn't 'mama.' It was 'pup-py.' The last excuse in my arsenal has been that we're in a rental house for two more months, but I called our landlord on my way over here." She sighed heavily. "He said yes, we can have a dog."

"What kind of dog do you want?"

She thought about it. "Sweet-natured. I don't like yippy, neurotic dogs. I've seen lovely furnishings destroyed by dogs that go berserk if they're left alone for a couple hours. And I don't like to see people put their dogs up to the table and coo about little Snookie-Snookums, with his hair in velvet bows, wanting his steak on fine china."

She pursed her lips and said, in baby-talk, "Mister Snookie doesn't know he's a dog. He thinks he's a human."

Jack laughed. "I think that says more about the people than the dogs."

She laughed, too. "True. I'm prepared to love a dog to distraction, but, hey—'You're a dog. Get off the couch.'"

"What size dog?"

"Medium. I think I have a prejudice about small dogs. Unfair though that may be, I like larger dogs. Border Collies, Australian Shepherds, although from what I read those breeds need to work. I don't want to get a dog and then have to buy a flock of sheep to entertain her."

"Pure breed, or a mutt?"

"Either. Sweet nature is most important. Loyal to a fault. Must love children. Must eat dog food. In a bowl. On the floor."

"I think this match is made in heaven."

"I beg your pardon?"

He grinned, and she realized he was speaking only of dogs. Hard to remember when he smiled like that. Even harder when she recalled what his lips felt like against hers.

"The match," he said with an undeniable sparkle in his eyes, "of Savannah, and you, and a dog. The puppies at the Randolph's farm are half Golden Retriever and half mystery mutt. Roy Randolph's best guess is the old half-blind, half-lame red heeler who lives a mile or so up the road is still more of a man than anyone gave him credit for."

She sighed. "Why does that make me think of my father?"

Jack laughed. "Actually, it makes me think of myself. I'm not getting any younger."

For a moment, she joined his laughter, but they both stopped. The silence was a little bit uncomfortable.

"Did I say something wrong?" he asked.

"No. Nothing. I got stuck thinking about my dad. Married. To Giselle. If I'd had any say about it, and obviously I didn't, I would have found him a nice widow, close to his age. And—"

She steepled her fingers against her lips, looking for the right words. "And I'm afraid that someday I'll be one of the older women who gets passed over for the post-pubescent sexpots. There! I said it." She looked at the floor, hating the way her cheeks burned. Why did she talk to Jack this way? Like he was...an old friend.

He probably thinks I'm unstable. Or—even worse—that I'm coming on to him.

She stood suddenly. "On that note of silliness, I'm going up to the attic to look for gold. Or fool's gold."

Jack put what was left of his sandwich back in the bag, brushed the breadcrumbs off his hand, and stood. "If you're looking for a fool, kiss me."

She leaned toward him as if drawn by a magnet. "I've only known you since Monday."

Whatever his answer, she lost it in their kiss. Their second kiss. And, oh, it was better than the first. Because this time he folded her against his all-male, all-muscle body.

I should back away. I should not keep kissing him.

Then again, I'm not getting any younger, either.

She slid her arms sinuously around his neck and opened her mouth to his tongue.

He explored, pressed, then pulled away to laugh. "I hope you don't take this wrong, but I think you're a post-pubescent sexpot."

"You silver-tongued devil." She smiled and turned her face to accept his kisses down her neck. Every nerve in her body was on full alert, especially those renegade nerves in her breasts.

"Mommy! Mommy, we're here."

Annie stepped back and called, "I'm up here, Savannah."

"I know how people have one baby," Jack murmured, "but I wonder how they ever have a second one." Loudly he called, "Marcy, I'm up here, too."

Annie reached out and wiped a lipstick smear from his cheek.

"Quick, let's get our story straight," he said. "Are you willing to go see the puppies tonight? Once Savannah sees them, you'll be under siege. Flaming arrows fired into the fort. You won't be able to say no."

"If we have puppies from the same litter, what does that make us? In-laws?"

"Out-laws."

"Jack, I don't know anything about house-training a puppy. Or anything else about training a puppy."

"I'll help you."

"Mommy, we fed carrots to the horses."

"And sugar lumps," Marcy added. "Right out of our hands."

They'd passed the second floor and were closing fast.

Annie rolled her eyes heavenward, and a groan escaped her lips. "All right, Jack. I'm in."

As Savannah and Marcy arrived on the third floor, Annie greeted Marcy and held out her arms to her daughter. "Wait until you hear the news, girlfriend."

Chapter Seven

Jack was in a time warp. All afternoon, time sped up and slowed down.

He was going to see Annie at seven o'clock. Would five o'clock ever get here? Six o'clock?

On the job, however, time flew. There was so much work to do, decisions to make and calls to return. The hardest part of a project like Albion House was keeping the workers working when one part of the project came to a sudden halt, awaiting an inspector or new materials. He thought of it as a river with partial dams around each bend. He had to spot alternative channels before the river backed up and flooded.

That was Jack's specialty, seeing hours and days ahead, laying out assignments on a white board and an Excel sheet. Without knowing it, he'd trained for this as a boy. From the time he was four until he was eight, his grandfather, Falco Cabrini, lived with them. In those last four years of his life, Falco had introduced Jack to his passion: the American Civil War.

The old man had almost four thousand toy soldiers, about half of them hand-painted by him. As Falco's health failed and he had to go on oxygen from a tank, first for a few hours a day, then twelve hours, then all the time, he drilled Jack on famous battles. Antietam, Shilo, Gettysburg. First Bull Run, Second Bull Run. The names of the generals, the layout of the fields, and the way each battle unfolded, became Jack's catechism. What should have happened, what could have happened, was as urgently discussed as the facts of what did happen.

If the general had sent for reinforcements, if the engineers had built a bridge in time, if they'd moved the gun emplacements earlier—everything in war was dependent on everything else.

The planner. The one who looked ahead. *He* was the winner.

Anyone seeing the old man and the boy lining up the companies and regiments—staging the battles on the plywood battlefield, with handcrafted mountains, rivers and bridges—might think the boy would grow up to be a soldier. Maybe even a general. But Jack had absorbed the lessons of his grandfather's passion and merged it with his father's passion for construction. In that, too, the planner was the winner.

Planning had nothing to do with love, however. A man could set his mind to find the right woman within six months—and die a bachelor forty years later. Conversely, he could make up his mind to die a bachelor, and get plucked like a Christmas goose before the month was up.

A woman could take perfect care of her health, never smoke, never do one thing wrong, and get lung cancer. Die at the age of thirty-two. Leave her eleven-year-old son and her husband bereft.

No, planning didn't always lead to good results. The race is not always to the swift, nor the battle to the strong. But it was the only compass Jack had.

While he moved his cement platoon to work on the garage, he sent a squad of carpenters to erect the small trusses on the covered walkway between the garage and the mudroom. While he pulled invoices out of the fax machine, he asked Gavin to call the county building inspector about the revised sewer line. In the middle of this, his phone rang. And threw a wrench in his cogs.

"Today?" he asked, incredulous. "You're getting here today?"

"Your stuff got loaded at the back of the truck,"

Ernie the mover said. "The loadmaster told you we couldn't guarantee Saturday delivery. I'll be in Bitter Falls in an hour and a half."

Jack stifled a groan and thanked Ernie for the heads up. He could have arrived in town and called from Jack's driveway.

"Tell you what," Ernie said, "I'll take my supper break before I drive out to your house. So I'll meet you there at four o'clock."

"Great, thanks." He hung up and looked at his white board. Knuckles Knudsen was working on the third floor.

He went upstairs and found Knuckles, waited for him to turn off the power saw, then explained his problem.

"You're in luck," Knuckles said. "My shift is over at three, and my cousin Tiny is over at Safeway. They put him on half time, so he needs the work. Baby on the way. Cash is king."

"That's three of us and the driver," Jack said. "I wonder if I should find another man to hire."

Knuckles laughed and slapped his thigh. "I guess you never seen Tiny, huh?"

Before he went downstairs, Jack climbed the ladder to the attic. "How's it going up here?"

"I was just about to call it done," Annie said. "Most of this junk will reduce the value of the town landfill, but I've got five things worth saving."

She pointed out two paintings she'd unwrapped and rewrapped to protect them. "I'll have to have them professionally cleaned and appraised for insurance, but I'm pretty sure they're by Charles Russell. Worth a fortune."

She'd also found a small table made of the burl of black walnut, and a silk-lined box of hotel memorabilia from San Francisco. "Pre-earthquake. My heart stopped when I opened it."

The last item was a steamer trunk with Goldie's black travel dress.

"The museum director will weep to see this," she said. "I can't be sure, but it looks like the dress Goldie was wearing in the picture the Seattle newspaper took of her, in 1896. They have the photo enlarged at the museum. The material is too fragile for me to take it out and show you, but they'll know how to display it at the museum."

"Have you looked at the letters yet?"

When Savannah and Marcy arrived, Annie had gathered up the papers she'd been studying and carried them to her car. He knew she was eager to see what answers they might contain.

She shook her head. "This took precedence. As soon as Tess and the girls left, I came up here. And thank heaven I did. As soon as we take these things to my car, you can do whatever you want with the attic."

"Good, let's do it now."

Together they carried the paintings to the top of the ladder, and he carried them down. The box of memorabilia and the walnut table were easy to retrieve, but he asked Knuckles to help him with the steamer trunk. It wasn't the weight that made it tricky; it was making sure the surface didn't get scraped as they passed it through the narrow opening.

The three of them got the treasure into her Ford Escape, and Knuckles went back to the third floor.

Jack watched Annie drive away. She'd said no to dinner; she was determined to read as much of the correspondence as she could. But she'd said, with a sparkle in her eyes that made him want to kiss her in front of God and everyone, that she'd see him at seven, at the Randolph's farm.

He laughed and put his hands on his hips. He was going to enjoy watching Savannah meet the puppies as much as Annie was.

*****

We'll get to Seattle late Thursday.

Tomorrow? Oh, yes, that's right. Thursday is tomorrow.

Annie's quick conversation with Delia Phinney played over in her head. The meeting with Sheldon Roth and his lawyer was set for ten a.m. Friday. She and Savannah would be on the twelve-ten plane back to Missoula.

When Annie arrived at the house on Maple Street, she carried Goldie's paintings, her box of San Francisco memorabilia, and the sheaf of correspondence from Goldie's attorneys into the house. As soon as she poured a glass of iced tea, she dug into the letters.

It was a story of strangers, and yet not all of the characters were strangers. She and Tess had heard some of the "middle story," the part that involved their mom, already.

All of Diana Brown Riker's attempts to identify her birth parents had failed. If she'd been adopted through an agency, she could have found the records. Using tools for adoption searches on the internet, Annie and Tess had searched, too.

Nothing. Dead ends. A baby girl, three days old, appeared out of nowhere in a house on the edge of the San Francisco Tenderloin district. Twice, when Annie visited Tess at the Marriott where she worked as assistant front desk manager, the two of them had looked for the second address of Diana's adoptive family. The first house had been bulldozed and the lot paved over for a parking lot many years ago. The second had been wiped off the map in a winter landslide.

The baby was named Diana Marie Brown by the adoptive parents, Sally and Logan Brown. Her original birth certificate said she'd been born at home with a nurse-midwife in attendance. Mother's name was handwritten and illegible; Joan, perhaps, or Jane. Last name started with an L. Lee? Age was eighteen. Father was listed as unknown.

Diana's adoptive father and mother had moved to California from Tennessee. Logan died when she was a teenager, and her adoptive mom suffered from early-onset Alzheimer's disease and died when Diana was twenty-three. The two aunts Diana knew of in Tennessee, half-sisters of Sally, answered her letters, but it was no help. They never even knew she was adopted.

She'd put it out of her mind and concentrated on her own family. And that was where the story lay, until Diana got sick and her daughters took up the search on her behalf.

While Diana was terminally ill with cancer, Annie flew to San Francisco and, using property tax records, tracked down the landlady from the Brown's second home. Diana remembered she'd called her Aunt Esther even though she was African-American and no relation. Esther had taken care of Diana and several other children to make extra money.

Annie found Esther Washington at a Goodwill Industries store where she worked three days a week. Esther recalled Diana Brown quite well and said she could see her features "plain as day" on Annie's face.

"I'm sorry to hear about the cancer," the old woman said. "She was always the sweetest little girl, always dressed neat as a pin. That child could not abide dirt. Only little girl I ever saw that could put on a pinafore in the morning and take it off at night just as clean. A reader, that one. Nobody had to teach her how to read. I think she was born knowing how. Always had her face in a book."

Against all odds, Esther knew something about Diana's birth parents. "Her mother was a bitty little thing, that's what Miz Brown told me. Girl thought the daddy would marry her. Didn't have no family to help. Back then it was different if a girl got pregnant, no husband. Not like it is now." She gave a snort of derision. "Movie stars have babies by three or four men and don't marry any of them. And they're proud of it. Hell's bells, a mother dog can do that."

Annie had swallowed a painful lump in her throat. She was due in five weeks and not married. The difference was, when she got pregnant, she'd thought she was married.

"I guess," she said to Esther, "the father wouldn't marry her after all?" She'd held her breath, closer than ever to the history her mother sought.

"No, ma'am. He went to Africa. That's what his mama said."

"His...his mother? Diana's grandmother?"

"Oh, yes, Miz Greta, I think was her name. I don't recall ever hearing her other name. I know she was a widow, like I was, and she didn't have two nickels to rub together."

Questions had crowded Annie's mind and spilled out of her mouth. Who, what, when, where? And...why?

Why had Diana's mother given her up?

"That's the easy one," Esther replied. Her eyes were kindly, and Annie's eyes filled with tears to think of her mom sitting on the lap of this woman.

"Please, tell me whatever you remember," she'd said.

"Miz Greta said the girl was out to trap her son, to make him marry her. I believed that malarkey for about one minute, and that was two minutes too long. Miz Brown told me the mama was a sweet girl who had nowhere to turn. Her name was Joan, if memory serves. She gave the baby to Miz Brown and her husband, and she moved away, said she was going to finish her schooling and get a good job someday."

"Do you know where she went?" Annie's hand went to her belly. Her heart ached for young, unmarried Joan. Giving birth, holding her infant in her arms, and then turning her back. Joan had to believe adoption by the Browns was the baby's best chance for a good life.

Esther squinted, then shook her head. "No, I never knew, or else I forgot."

Annie had flown back to Seattle and told what little she'd learned to her mom. Diana, wearing a scarf wrapped like a turban on her bald head, sat on the couch. She'd told Annie and Tess all she remembered of Aunt Esther. No, she had no memory of a grandmother named Greta.

Now, setting her iced tea on her bedside table and getting comfortable against the headboard, Annie picked up documents from the 1930s.

Goldie had written to her son Stanley in 1938, demanding that he return home to Montana. He'd moved—or "run off," as Goldie put it in letters to her attorney—in 1935, at the age of twenty-seven, to work for the railroad. Now, according to Greta, he'd taken up with a "dance hall floozy."

Through Leopold Dusart—there was only one "Dusart" on the law firm's door at that time—Goldie hired a detective to track down "the truth" about the "loose woman" who was "after Stanley's money."

According to the report by the detective, Stanley met a buxom beauty, Greta Bauer, at a dance hall in early 1938. Greta was the middle child in a family dance troupe who traveled on the vaudeville circuit. In the depth of the Great Depression, she dropped out of the troupe and worked as a waitress and pay-to-dance girl in the Tenderloin.

Goldie used what little derogatory information the detective dug up, namely that Greta's oldest brother was in prison for manslaughter, to blacken her name. Stanley wouldn't listen.

In fact, her tactic backfired. Instead of gradually giving in, Stanley refused to open mail from his increasingly shrill mother. Leopold Dusart went in person to tell Stanley that if he married Greta, his mother would "cut him off." Disinherit him.

Stanley told Dusart to get out of his apartment. He said he loved Greta and he would live his life without interference by his mother, and attorneys, and detectives.

The next day he married Greta. Until his death in 1947, he never spoke to or wrote to his mother.

Goldie left her will intact but was too proud to let Stanley know it. Dusart notified her of the birth of her grandson, Luke Jones, in 1940, and of the birth and death of a second grandson in 1942. She had her will rewritten after Stanley's death. In addition to generous provisions for her sister, Violet, she said that Albion House, the land surrounding it, and most of her fortune would go to Luke when she died.

She knew Greta and young Luke lived in abject poverty, but she was so bitter about Stanley's disobedience, so convinced that Greta had bewitched him, that she wouldn't help them.

Predictably, Greta's bitterness at being so maligned and ill-used by Stanley's mother hardened her heart against Goldie. Annie had a picture in her mind of two stone lions on library steps.

As far as the record showed, Greta never told Luke who his father's mother was. Luke could have grown up to be kind, the sort of boy who gets a job as soon as possible to take care of his mother. But, instead, he grew up cold and self-centered—and as adventurous as his grandmother had been when she was his age.

His plan to go to Africa was delayed when his girlfriend, a Russian Hill housemaid named Joan Lee, ended up pregnant. At his mother's insistence, he stayed in San Francisco until the baby was born.

Dusart's detective wrote to Goldie that Luke saw the baby, said it was "red as a damn Indian." He told the girl he was never coming back, and she might as well give the baby away. A few hours later, he was on board a freighter.

Annie shook her head in disgust and drank some tea. Apparently, Luke Jones didn't leave his heart, or anything else that could help his baby daughter, in San Francisco.

The trail ended there. The girl, Joan Lee, disappeared without a trace. Dusart and the detective hired people to get close to Greta and find out where the baby went. But she never said a word.

Through the U.S. State Department, Dusart and Dusart tracked Luke Jones. He was a soldier of fortune and later a farmer in South Africa. He had no more children. When he died in South Africa in 1980, the same year Violet died in Montana, Goldie changed her will for the last time. She left Violet's share of her estate to Violet's heirs, and her son Stanley's share to the natural born child of Luke Jones and Joan Lee.

A girl. Date of birth, August 10, 1960. Place of birth, San Francisco. Name, unknown. Residence, unknown.

Annie set the documents on the dining room table and stared without focus toward her dresser, at a stack of reference books on interior design. She went into the kitchen, poured another glass of iced tea, and cut up a Fuji apple.

She'd started reading the mystery in the middle, gone back to the beginning. Now she had to know the ending. How did Goldie's attorneys find Annie and Tess Riker?

She returned to her bedroom and picked up the last folder.

Greta remarried in 1957, ten years after Stanley died. Three years before "baby girl" was born and Luke left for Africa. The marriage seemed to be successful, and it lifted her out of poverty. Her second husband also preceded her in death, in 1982. When Greta Jones O'Shay died, in 1994, her stepdaughter moved into the house. Leopold Dusart III, acting for the estate of the late Goldie Jones, tried to buy all of Greta's personal effects. The stepdaughter refused. Dusart reported to his partners that the woman clearly suffered from an obsession to hold onto all possessions, no matter how difficult it became to move inside the house.

Again they waited. Annie noted, wryly, that they billed the estate regularly. Every time anyone so much as said "Goldie," there was an invoice. Year in, year out.

The attorneys called it loyalty. To Annie it looked more like a pride of lions guarding a carcass until they felt like eating more.

At last, two years ago, the stepdaughter died. Riley Dusart had already negotiated with the cousin who would "inherit" the firetrap and be required by the county to clean it out within fifteen days. For one-tenth of what his father had offered the stepdaughter, Leo bought all of Greta's household effects. A few hours after he and an assistant arrived at the modest Oakland, California, home, they left with the backseat of his car filled with paperwork. Everything else was removed by disaster clean-up experts and carried to the town landfill.

Part of the deal with the cousin was that Dusart and Dusart would have the empty house fumigated. Then it was hers to do with as she wished.

He'd had to fumigate his car, too. All duly noted on invoices, as were what was by then an astronomical number of billable hours. For Leopold Dusart and his heirs, Goldie Jones had truly been the gift that kept on giving.

Paralegals worked in a motel room and then a conference room at the firm. When they had all the detritus sorted and catalogued, the detective agency took the case to its conclusion. The heir Goldie was seeking was dead, but Diana Brown Riker had left two daughters.

Letter written. Invoice prepared. Fee paid. The End.

And, at the same time, a new beginning.

She put aside the information about Diana's birth mother, Joan Lee, whom Greta had kept track of after she moved to Dayton, Ohio, and married. She'd stayed in touch once or twice a year with the adoptive parents, too.

Joan had married and had a son and a daughter. Diana's half-sister and half-brother. They'd stayed in Ohio and each had three children. Cousins, biologically, to Annie and Tess.

She heard the sound of Tess's car in the driveway and went out the front door, expecting to have a chattering Savannah hopping out of the backseat. Instead, only Tess got out.

"Where are the girls?"

"The ranch has a pottery painting class this afternoon. They're both signed up."

Annie laughed. "Maybe I should rent a cabin at the Rocking Star. Savannah has made herself at home out there."

"Let's go inside," Tess said.

"What?" There was something in Tess's voice that made Annie uneasy.

"It's nothing bad. I just wanted to talk to you without interruption. We're both so busy..."

"You want some tea? Or iced coffee? I have some in the refrigerator."

"No, thanks." She walked into the house, and Annie followed.

Tess had said it was nothing bad, but the hair was still up on the back of Annie's neck. The two of them were as close as shadows. Best friends. "What's up?"

"You have probably noticed that I'm spending time with Tree Autrey." A grin teased at the corners of her mouth and widened. "Well...he's asked me to marry him, and I said yes."

"That's wonderful!" She threw her arms around Tess's shoulders and squeezed. "I hope he knows that makes him the luckiest man on earth."

"He mentioned something along that line."

"When? You have to have a real wedding. Don't run off somewhere, please."

She saw a shadow cross Tess's face and knew exactly what she was thinking. *Don't run off like I did. Don't come back from Hawaii and drop da bomb.*

"We'll have a real wedding, but it will be small."

"We can use the gazebo—"

"The gazebo won't be ready in time. We'll get married at the ranch. On June twenty-first. Midsummer night."

"That's only four weeks from now! Are you insane?" She hugged Tess again. "Of course you are. Falling in love is insanity."

Slowly, she let her arms fall away, and she backed up two steps. "Oh, my. Oh, my, oh my."

The enormity of what Tess had said finally dawned on her. They'd moved to Bitter Falls to run a bed and breakfast with special accommodations for weddings and reunions. Annie, and Tess, and Savannah, and Dad. But Dad had bailed, and now Tess was bailing, too.

Tears pooled in Annie's eyes and spilled down her cheeks. "I'm sorry, Tess. I can't help crying. I can't—I can't do this alone. First Duke, and then Dad, and now you."

The people I want close are pulling away, she thought, causing another gusher of tears. *And Peter Dylan, the last man I ever want to see, is back in my life.*

"Tree and I have been talking about Albion House," Tess said. "Hold on." She found a box of tissues on the kitchen counter and pulled out eight or nine.

Annie took the wad of tissues and pressed it to her face.

"Come on, sit down." Tess tugged on Annie's hand until she moved toward the couch. The house phone rang, but they ignored it.

"It's overwhelming, Tess. I can't do it alone."

"Just because I'll be living five miles out of town doesn't mean I won't be a full partner."

"I'm sorry. I'm being selfish."

Tess pulled an ottoman in front of Annie and sat on it. She took her free hand in hers and squeezed. "Listen, all our bookings are done online and by phone. How many people have contacted us for a job, huh? When the construction is complete, Albion House can run like clockwork. I never intended to bake muffins and clean toilets. And you don't have to do that either."

"Coming here was my idea." Annie blew her nose. "It was always seventy-five percent what I wanted and twenty-five percent what you wanted."

"Well, I'm one hundred percent here now. I've found the love of my life, and we're going to start a family. The sooner the better. Savannah will have cousins."

"She'll be out of her mind with excitement. A wedding."

"Well, yes, a wedding is fun, but it's not as good as a puppy."

"That's another thing. I have to train the puppy with no help from you."

"Didn't *Jack* say he'd help?" Tess stretched out his name. "That sounds like a better deal to me."

Annie's cell phone rang. She glanced at her caller ID and shrugged. "Business. I'll call back."

Tess's phone rang. She turned it off without looking. "I have to go."

"I know. We're—we're always on the run, aren't we?" She didn't intend to sound sad, but it came out that way. She shrugged and made an attempt to laugh. "Maybe I should have some cheese with my whine."

"You're entitled to a whine now and then. Especially when you have to face down Sheldon-

Peter-Dylan-Roth the day after tomorrow. I'll come with you."

"No. I can do this. Delia has it under control. Ten minutes. As soon as the jerk leaves the country, I'll feel like I have my life back."

Annie's cell phone and the house phone rang at the same time. She looked at the number. "I'd better take it this time."

"I'll get the other one," Tess said.

Ten minutes later, after a hug, and another hug, and another hug in the driveway, Tess drove away.

Annie realized she hadn't told her what she'd discovered about Great-great-grandmother Goldie. And Great-grandmother Greta. And Grandmother Joan, the birth mother Diana never found.

The whole story, now that she knew it, was too sad to dwell on. She'd thought she would admire Greta, the woman Stanley loved enough to defy his mother. But Greta turned out to be just as unforgiving as Goldie, hiding the identity of Luke's daughter from Goldie all the way to her grave. For years beyond her grave, in fact.

Bitter Falls got its name from Indians or French trappers before Lewis and Clark. The origin was murky. But it could just as well have been named for the fabulously wealthy and perpetually bitter woman who built a mansion looking over the town one hundred years ago.

Albion House needed more than a facelift. It needed a heart. It needed laughter and...happiness.

The immortal words of a great American philosopher, Charlie Brown, came into her mind, and a laugh whooshed out of her like air out of a balloon.

Happiness is a warm puppy.

Chapter Eight

"Tony Al wants us off the case." Deputy U.S. Marshal Mike Hale popped his knuckles, a new bad habit he'd taken up to replace smoking. He also chewed bubble gum; another annoying *pop* when she least expected it.

"Tony Alberghetti," Susan Hightower said, using his full name as if it left a foul taste in her mouth, which, come to think of it, was true, "is transferring to the FBI. He wants whatever they want. He'd like to carry it to them in his teeth."

"I know." Mike shrugged as he unlocked their car in the secure parking area. "He's a jerk. But C. Edgar Sommers loves him like a son. I hear he's approving the transfer so he'll have more chance for career advancement."

At the Tuesday staff meeting, some twenty-four hours ago, it had been all Susan could do to keep her mouth shut. She'd written INSUBORDINATION on her yellow pad and then drawn boxes, circles, and arrows around the word.

Since then, she'd worked at the edges of the Sheldon Roth case, like a runt piglet trying to get at the milk dispensers.

I'll suck hind tit. No problem! Just give me a chance.

"What are you thinking?" Mike asked. "Spill."

She looked at her watch. Four o'clock. "Head toward Qwest Field. Thank goodness there's not a home game, or we wouldn't get close to this address."

She gave him a number on Alaskan Way.

"In the list of people who Roth called regularly," she said, "I found a phone number that's very odd. I called it from an outside phone. The man is a photographer and videographer. Josef Abbas. He was polite but said whoever told me to call was mistaken. He doesn't do weddings. He works for lawyers. I checked further and found that he worked on Sheldon Roth's defense."

"Yeah. And?"

"I looked back at information I compiled while U.S. Marshals and the Bellevue P.D. were watching Roth, then known as Peter Dylan, before the arrest. He had a corporate account with the photographer. I reached the detective who questioned Abbas, and it was a dead end."

"Now comes the *however*," Mike said with a snicker.

Susan nodded. "However, I wanted to know why Abbas was accepting collect calls from Shelly in prison. So I asked the warden and got passed from lieutenant to sergeant. The librarian who is in charge of the computers—"

"Please don't tell me Roth had access to computers."

"He was one of twenty inmates who were employed and paid small amounts of money to give out prepared information about Oregon parks, how to reserve a spot, and phone numbers of private campgrounds. He didn't make reservations; he just told people how to do it. As an ambassador for the state of Oregon, he answered the phone and used the computer. The lieutenant told me it was all supervised."

"But if they screwed up, or if he paid off somebody in the system and managed to use a computer for his purposes, they'll hide it behind the moon. Am I right?"

She nodded. "After we talk to Abbas, let's figure out where the Feebs have stashed Shelly. I know from Delia Phinney, Annie Riker's lawyer, that he's supposed to be singing like the proverbial canary. In return, he gets a new passport and a ride to the airport."

"When?"

"Like they'll tell me? Friday afternoon at the earliest. At ten a.m., Annie Riker and her little girl have to show up. Command performance. Otherwise he won't sign the doc to relinquish parental rights. Ms. Phinney and I will be there."

"You? How'd that happen?"

"Oh, I thought I'd told you. I offered my services to Ms. Phinney, and she said yes. It's the least I can do." She grumbled. "And with the FBI strong-arming us, the *least* I can do is the *most* I can do."

"Well, at least they didn't stick him in Wit-Sec," Mike said. "Get him a job in Peoria and make U.S. Marshals shine his shoes for thirty years."

"He's got a better deal. I just wish to hell I knew what it is. Money, money, money, money. And I wonder where Judge Walter Sommers is."

"Ask his brother. C. Edgar must know. He wouldn't tell you, but it would be entertaining to watch his face turn the color of tomato soup."

"Yeah." She looked out the window. "Delia Phinney's guess was that Shelly's release had something to do with the arrest of Judge Herbert Magnusson, but now it looks like the two events are simply coincidental."

"How's that?"

"I have a friend in Spokane who says Magnusson flamed out the old-fashioned way. Child pornography on his federal judiciary computer."

"How come that's not in the news?" Mike raced through an intersection on the yellow light.

"They're trying to break a lucrative porno ring among professionals. My friend says Magnusson is, uh, cooperating."

She used the time in transit to look again through papers she'd retrieved by computer and printed out.

"Should be in this block," Mike said.

"I see a parking place. Let's go ask some questions."

Forty minutes later, they stood on the sidewalk and looked up at the concrete walls of Qwest Field looming over them.

"Son of a bitch," Susan said.

"You got that right." Mike popped his knuckles.

"How are we going to get access to a computer at a federal prison in Oregon?"

"It's pointless," Mike said. "There won't be anything there. If there were a case, which there isn't, the prosecution could subpoena this guy. Make him testify that he was paid to take pictures of Sheldon Roth's biological daughter."

Susan got in the driver's seat. "Shelly would cry about wanting to see what 'my little girl' looked like. I'm sure Annie Riker refused to send a photo. But why did he do it?"

"Why did he pay for pictures?"

"Yes. Why did he want to see them? It's been proven beyond the shadow of a doubt that he has no heart in his chest cavity, never did, never will. So why the interest in Savannah? It makes my skin crawl."

She slapped the steering wheel. "Annie's lawyer will scream bloody murder." She gave her phone to Mike along with Delia's business card. "Tell her I have to talk to her tonight."

He dialed and left the message. "Now what? I hope you're going to say supper. I skipped lunch to go to another hypnosis session."

"We've got to get across the bridge before the traffic gets any worse. We can eat at Roscoe's."

"Where the Feebs go? I thought you hated that place."

"I do. But I might find out where they've stashed Shelly. And the news of Walter Sommers sudden retirement is out on the street by now. We might hear something. I'll use my charm."

Mike laughed. "You are smart and gorgeous, Susan, and the best marksman in Seattle, but you are never charming."

"I've just never tried," she said archly. "And how hard can it be, Michael? *You're* charming."

Vera said, "and Savannah. She's a bundle of , isn't she, Jack?"

t of sight of Annie, Vera looked Annie up and nd gave Jack a wink and a thumbs up sign.

y Randolph crossed the yard, calling his e to Marcy. Big, raw-boned and tan from seventy years of farming, Roy greeted Jack handshake and met Vera and Annie for the me. As they followed the girls to the barn, he ow glad everyone in Bitter Falls was to see House get a new lease on life.

ith the Suncatcher Factory running two and expanding their space, and the new state branch growing, and now Albion House g back from the dead, Bitter Falls is quite the town," he said. "It doesn't hurt to add five women to the population."

ive?" Vera asked.

m including you, of course," Roy said. "A man e appreciates a lady with seasoning."

era laughed and transferred her hand from arm to Roy's. "A woman my age appreciates a with his own teeth."

oy threw back his head and roared with ter.

ack and Annie exchanged a knowing look.

Uh-oh, here comes trouble," Roy said. "How pups do you folks want, anyway?"

avannah and Marcy emerged from the barn. had two wriggling monkey-pups in her arms, all of the pups wanted to go in the same tion, up and over the girls' shoulders.

Mommy," Savannah called in a paroxysm of joy, puppies like me!"

nnie dashed forward to catch the one that was ing by its back legs and scratching fiercely at nnah's back. As soon as she took possession, the tried to crawl up and over her shoulder, and e of twenty seconds she was in the same fix

Chapter Nine

Jack drove Vera's sedan down the long driveway of the Randolph farm and parked behind an unattached horse trailer. Vera had protested that she didn't "need to come," but he'd insisted.

"Do it to assuage my guilt," he'd said. "I promised we'd have more quality time together once we moved to Montana, and I've hardly seen you."

He could tell, beneath her protest, that she was glad to be included. He and Marcy were her family.

The life of Jack Cabrini had improved beyond measure since they'd arrived in Montana. There were just two clouds over it. The first was worry about Marcy getting dragged into testifying against Luella DeBeers, her vicious daughter Crystal, and Crystal's equally nasty sidekick, Heather Janson.

Travis McGarry had called him mid-afternoon to say the district attorney's office was quieter than King Tut's tomb. Quieter, in fact, than Mile High Stadium on Super Bowl Sunday.

Jack's other worry was for Annie and Savannah. This time tomorrow, they'd be on their way to Missoula to catch a plane to Seattle. The next morning Annie would face down the charmer who'd taken advantage of her, two other women at the very least, and more than fifty sophisticated investors. When word got out that Sheldon Roth was out of prison and walking off scot-free, there would be wailing and gnashing of teeth in the Emerald City. He hoped some of the teeth would gnash into "Sheldon's" thick hide and rip some of it off.

Why hadn't the FBI tracked down his money? Correction, not *his* money. The money that belonged to the investors? They'd had about six months between his arrest and trial, plus another five and a half years. Or had they found some of it, and wanted to quietly keep it for the FBI? The whole business stunk like bloated road kill.

From the backseat, Marcy asked Vera about her hip surgery, adding, "I can come stay with you after your operation. I'll do all the cooking."

"That's very sweet, Marcy, and I know you could handle the job, but my sister is coming from Denver. I'm trying to talk her into a long visit, and if you're there doing everything for me, she'll say, 'I guess I'm not needed here,' and she'll be on the next train out of Montana. No, let's give her plenty to do."

"Well," Marcy said, "I wouldn't want her to leave too soon. But I'll come see you and bring you cookies."

"That will be fine. And read to me. My cataracts are giving me fits."

"More surgery?" Jack asked.

"Sometime, yes. No rush. Nothing to worry about."

"Wait till you see my puppy, Aunt Vera." Marcy got out and opened the front door for her. "She's so soft. Her little tongue is the sweetest thing. She looks like this." She put her hands up to her chin, fingers forward like limp paws, and stuck her tongue out and in rapidly.

"She looks like a lizard?" Jack asked. "When they said they didn't know who her father is, I never guessed it was a Komodo dragon."

"Ha, ha, ha," Marcy said dismissively.

"Here come Annie and Savannah," Jack said. He rolled his shoulders around, trying to work out a kink in his neck. Knuckles Knudsen and his cousin "Tiny" had carried the heaviest furniture in like it was made out of balsa wood. The driver worked at about half-speed and carried the lightest boxes he could find. Jack hauled boxes marked "Bedroom"

and "Bathroom," and the frame up the stairs. As soon as he'd a and bolted it to the headboard, springs and mattress into place.

Vera had picked up Marcy brought her out to help. The two shelf paper and lined drawers a the kitchen well on the way to us Jack got the appliances hooked up

Instead of going back to the house, Jack, Marcy and Vera had supper in the new house, lasag microwave plus vegetables steam range.

Ever since he'd seen the ho offer, Jack's mind had danced opening up the kitchen and makin cooking island. Marcy was crazy a he'd bought duplicates of the ap Denver kitchen and had them deli The arrangement as it was now c but he couldn't remodel his house Albion House.

After a quick supper, he unpacked towels, toiletries, and f enjoyed once again the luxury of two

Annie pulled her Ford Escape i and stepped out. She wore a full ski and a pale blue blouse off the shoul her kissable neck to advantage.

"Savannah, come with me," M Jack had taken her place beside Ve raced pell-mell to the barn.

"Laughing all the way," Vera m never hear too much of that."

Jack introduced Vera to Annie, it was a pleasure to get summer storage.

"I've already had the pleasure

Savannah had been.

It was Jack's turn to affect a rescue. He held the squirmer out in front of him to protect his bare arms from the claws. "I think these guys have doubled in size in a week. When do they learn they can't fly?"

As if on cue, one of Marcy's broke free of her grasp and did a forward one-and-a-half on the way to the ground. Marcy shrieked that he was hurt.

Roy Randolph scooped him up without breaking his stride. "He's okay. I think he's made out of rubber." He held the little guy up to his face and rubbed noses.

An hour later, the girls were playing with their designated pups, sisters they'd named Lady and Katy. Both were silky and looked pretty much like their mom, but with more red in their coloring. The other four pups had shorter, more wiry hair and sharper noses. The six of them had two goals in life, so far. To coerce their mother into nursing them, and to bite each other's tails, ears, and necks in fierce combat.

Savannah had been distressed at the wrestling and biting, not believing that they weren't hurting each other. She'd pull one away, and he or she would spring back like a Slinky, eager to continue the mauling. From time to time one would yip and hop backward.

At last they'd fallen asleep and the girls held their temporarily docile pets, saying over and over how soft they were.

Roy had invited them all to stay for homemade ice cream, "later," and Vera went inside the white farmhouse with him.

After a day that had raced headlong out of the starting gate and gone around the track more times than he could count, Jack was ready to sit on a bench in Roy's sunflower garden and listen to the evening sounds of birds. Sitting close beside Annie, he felt...contentment. He took her hand in his and threaded their fingers together.

"Listen," he said.

"What? I don't hear anything."

"That's what I mean. I don't hear planes, helicopters, eighteen-wheelers, horns, or sirens. Just birds. And I think I hear Roy's vegetables growing."

She laughed. "I think that's the sound of Lady and Katy growing. Did you see the size of their paws? And speaking of things that mushroom before our very eyes, Tess and Tree Autrey are getting married June twenty-first. She told me this afternoon."

"Tree? Tree Autrey, the confirmed bachelor?" he asked incredulously. "How did I miss the signs?" What he didn't say—but thought—was, *He's older than I am!*

"I guess I don't even know what the signs are in my own sister. I had no idea they were so close." She sighed. "Of course, I'm very, very happy for them. But I had a selfish reaction about four seconds after she told me. What about running Albion House? Tess says she'll always be a full partner, and she pointed out that a lot of people want to work there. But I might as well face it—I'm up a creek with no paddle in sight."

"You're worried about Seattle, aren't you? What time do you leave?"

"Our plane leaves Missoula tomorrow evening, at seven-thirty. We'll stay at a hotel near the courthouse, which is also near Isaac Chenoweth's office. We'll go directly from there to the airport. I don't want to stay in Peter's force field one minute longer than necessary."

He put his arm around her shoulder and kissed her forehead. "You and I have a lot in common. We both moved to Bitter Falls to find safety for kids, and we've both been followed by trouble."

"I'm listening." She relaxed against him, and he relished the faint citrus fragrance of her shampoo.

He was struck by the turnabout of their positions. Only last night, beside the pond at the Rocking Star, he'd been the one urging Annie to talk, and she'd spilled out the story of her less-than-legal marriage to a man who called himself Peter Dylan.

"I'm waiting for the other boot to fall," he said, "just like you are. I left Denver to get Marcy out of a social and legal quagmire. She went to an expensive day school, and she hated it, but I was so wrapped up in Great Western that I blew off her complaints."

"What kind of complaints?"

He shrugged. "The girls at her school were all wrapped up in having the best clothes. And by best, I mean the most expensive. Shopping and showing off weren't hobbies. They were blood sports. *Lord of the Flies* at Neiman-Marcus. I gave Marcy a credit card and expected her to buy whatever the 'in' clothes were. The thing is, I didn't believe her when she said all the girls were like that. It had to be an exaggeration."

He sighed and continued. "Well, it wasn't an exaggeration. Any girls who didn't worship the golden calf had transferred out. Marcy was the only meat in the Colosseum. They made her life hell. I said, 'Ignore them and spend your time studying. Get A's.' Ha. In addition to shopping, the girls and boys both had elevated cheating to unimaginable levels. Marcy couldn't get a break. And I was deaf."

"She must have been miserable," Annie said softly.

"Then things got worse." He paused. He hated to think about what had happened. How much harder had it been for Marcy to endure?

"Marcy was alone at Neiman-Marcus, three weeks before Christmas. She'd asked me to go with her to shop and have dinner out, but I was too busy. As usual. I told her to find what she wanted for Christmas and tell me about it. I figured I could make a call, have it delivered, and not miss any work. The perfect guy solution."

She chuckled, and he squeezed her shoulders. "I remember I had a trip coming up, to Portland to look at a job site. Two days, out and back. Vera was going to stay with Marcy, and I had a cleaning woman coming so Vera wouldn't overdo and hurt herself. It was all going to fall into place. Slick and efficient, just the way I liked things to work."

"But something happened to change that." She prodded him to continue.

"Yeah, something happened. Marcy got arrested for shoplifting."

"Oh, my."

"I got a call from the police, and I called my attorney, Travis McGarry, who's also my best friend, and I stormed downtown, full of righteous fury directed at the wrong person—at Marcy. I'll be grateful to my grave to Travis for stopping me before I did irreparable harm to her self-image. And to our relationship."

He stood and paced in front of the bench.

"Travis got to the jail ten seconds before I did, but it was enough. He got in my face, backed me against a wall, and told me to cool off before I made a big mistake. 'Before you go off half cocked,' he said, 'remember what happened the night you wrecked your dad's car.'"

He shook his head, still shamed by his initial reaction to Marcy's trouble.

"The night I turned seventeen, I ran my dad's car into a ditch, tore out the whole undercarriage. Totaled it. It was stupid, stupid, stupid. I'd been acting the fool, showing off, speeding." He sighed heavily. "I had worse judgment than a raccoon on an interstate highway. When my dad walked into the emergency room where I was getting six stitches, I expected him to call me a bonehead, a fool, maybe even an ass wipe. But, no. He put his arms around me and cried. *Cried!* Said, 'It's only a car. The important thing is, you're all right.'"

Annie stood and hugged him, kissing both cheeks.

"Thanks to that just-in-time reminder, I walked into the jail and took Marcy in my arms. If she'd made a mistake, we would live through it together. And if the police had made a mistake, Travis was there to tear them a new one."

"What happened?"

"Travis took Marcy to an interview room for five minutes. When he came out, he said his client was ready to be interviewed by the police. He would be in the room with her, and so would her brother and legal guardian. He reminded them to videotape the session. The detective had a big gotcha smirk on his face."

Jack folded Annie in his arms. "The arrogant grin was gone when the four of us came out of the room. Marcy had seen Crystal DeBeers and Heather Janson shoplift jewelry at Neiman-Marcus. Everything she said had happened was right there on the surveillance tape. The two of them had dropped jewelry in their coat pockets before they saw her. She was looking at cufflinks. For me, of course. They called her over and acted friendly. The jewelry saleswoman took the black velvet display off the counter before Marcy walked to that counter. When the saleswoman noticed a diamond bracelet and pearl earrings were missing, she called a plainclothes guard over. The two of them confronted the three girls—and Crystal and Heather slipped the jewelry out of their pockets and dropped it into Marcy's shopping bag."

"Oh, how horrible for her!"

"The three of them were taken to the store's security office, and Crystal and Heather threw the blame at Marcy. Crystal's mother, a barracuda named Luella DeBeers, showed up inside of fifteen minutes and took the two of them out of there.

Marcy was left all alone and was taken downtown in a police car."

Annie sat on the bench and he joined her, but his backbone was as rigid as his jaw. The muscles in the back of his neck that had been stiff before were on their way to painful spasms now. He rolled his head around and rubbed his neck.

"Once the police saw the surveillance tape," he said, "they knew the other girls had taken the jewelry and framed Marcy. The store got their jewelry back and didn't want any trouble with the DeBeers and Janson families, so the whole thing was dropped. That didn't stop Crystal and Heather from spreading the story at school, though. They used school computers to do it, too.

"Then it got even worse. Someone, not Marcy, sent an unsigned letter to the principal exposing the cyber-theft of math tests before a big test, by—guess who?—Crystal DeBeers. I suspect it was the math teacher who was afraid to confront the issue head on."

He leaned forward. With his elbows on his thighs, he rested his forehead on his hands. Annie reached over and began kneading the tight muscles in his neck and upper back. Then she walked around behind him and used both hands, making tight half circles with her thumbs, each circle toward his spine.

"What happened next?" she asked.

"Two things. More lies about Marcy spread via the school computers, and Luella DeBeers did pretty much the same thing as the infamous 'cyber bully mom' in Missouri. She created a fake Facebook page and repeated the lies that were going around the school."

"Poor Marcy. I'm twenty-nine, and I don't think I could stand up under that abuse."

"The thing is, Marcy didn't break down; she didn't crumble. She got more and more determined to fight back. It was hard to get her to back away.

Travis and I told her, it's a noble thing to tell the truth and expose evil, but Luella DeBeers and Heather Janson's parents, in addition, of course, to the little darlings, don't fight fair. Marcy would not only be taking a knife to a gunfight, she'd be taking a plastic knife to a bombing range. I got her out of there."

"So it's over?"

She continued making circles with the heels of her hands, and he could tell the muscles were beginning to relax.

"No. It's growing faster than Lady and Katy. Travis called me Monday to say the district attorney might be taking a case against Luella DeBeers to a grand jury. If so, Marcy might get dragged back into the rat's nest."

"What kind of case?"

"Well, grand juries keep it quiet. But Travis found out that Crystal, Heather and Luella—nicknamed Cruella in the media—pulled the same smear campaign against the son of a former United States Secretary of the Interior. The case is probably going to blow up. The school is named as a co-defendant because they allowed school computers to be used. Naturally, the district attorney wants all the facts of Marcy's harassment to come in."

"Marcy doesn't seem to be worried about anything. Have you not told her yet?"

He stopped her right hand, brought it around to his lips and kissed it. "I told her. She's chomping at the bit to testify. I think she saw *Erin Brockovich* too many times. She's been on the phone, trying to shake down Travis for details of the case. And as for Travis, I think he's been reading too many John Grisham novels. The two of them are probably working behind my back on strategy."

"And you want the whole thing to go away?"

He stood and took her in his arms again. "Those were my exact words to Travis. But it looks like—

again—I've underestimated my little sister."

Annie threaded her arms around his neck and kissed him on the cheeks, the mouth, and cheeks again. "You must be very proud of her."

He savored the feel of her body against his, aware that his response was becoming more obvious with each passing second.

"What were we talking about?" he murmured. Her mouth was so sweet. He nipped gently at her lower lip like a bee circling a flower.

She made a moaning sound and sighed. "Were we talking?"

He felt her mouth open to him, and he deepened the kiss.

"Mommy!" Savannah called. "Where are you?"

"Over here." Annie stepped away from Jack as she answered.

"Mommy, the ice cream is ready. Hurry! Mr. Randolph said we can put chocolate on top, and nuts."

Jack laughed. "Nuts, huh? That's what I was just about to say. Nuts!"

"By my count," Annie said softly, "we've had three single kisses. I wonder when we'll ever have two in a row?"

"Come see my house, tonight," he said. It had been a sudden idea, voiced before he'd thought about it. "I'll talk Vera into taking the girls to her house for an hour or so. Please?"

"Does any woman say no when you turn on the charm?"

"Ma'am, do you really want an answer to that question?"

She grinned. "All right. Your house, for one hour. After we have our ice cream."

"I'll bet I can eat ice cream in fifteen seconds. How about you?"

"Twelve seconds. We don't want anything to melt, do we?"

As they walked arm in arm toward the back door of the farmhouse, Jack listened to the sound of two girls, giggling.

Something is melting fast in Bitter Falls, Montana, he thought. *And it isn't ice cream.*

Chapter Ten

"How did you find this house?" Annie asked. "I love this."

The modern house was constructed of wood, metal and glass. The shape was irregular, conforming to the land instead of having the site bulldozed flat for a more conventional house. From outside it appeared to have three levels for living, plus a three-car garage built into the hillside. In the last light of the already set sun, the upper windows had a glow.

"Duke drove out to look at the owner's three German Max Blank stoves to see if we wanted to install one at Albion House. The distributor had arranged with the owner to show them."

While Jack spoke, he started a wood fire in an elegant freestanding fireplace. "This one is called the Mega Elegance II."

"Duke didn't mention them to me."

"No. As you see, they're too modern looking. Not a good fit with the look you're going with at Albion House."

She climbed six stairs to a nook lined with bookshelves that would make a terrific reading area. Naturally, she thought about Jack and his "mulled wine and stack of good books."

Slowly, she walked around a gunmetal gray oval stove. "This one is amazing."

"That's the Berlin model," he said. "It can be rotated around that vent pipe, so you can sit where you want and still face the fire. I have a set of curved sofas on order for that area. The third fireplace unit is in the garage. The previous owner hadn't installed it yet, and I'm going to remodel the whole kitchen, so it has to wait."

She returned to the main level and crossed the wide central space that shared a cedar tongue and groove cathedral ceiling with the dining room and the "mezzanine" reading area. Near the kitchen, she found the door to the garage. Down more stairs, she studied the third ultramodern stove. At first glance, she thought it was an odd triple oven with its three metal cubes, each with a side-opening door.

Jack came down the stairs, too. "Wood is stored in the bottom, the firebox is in the middle, and the compartment on the top is a working oven."

"What's this one called?" She ran her fingers down the tiles on the side of the units.

"The Florenz. When Duke drove out here, the house wasn't for sale, but shortly after that the owner suddenly decided to move to Whitefish. So much more trendy, don't you know? These stoves and several other features he'd added to the house are more expensive than buyers generally are willing to pay. Wait till you see the Hollywood-style hot tub outside the master bedroom suite. So, you see, he'd put himself in a bind, market-wise. But then—along came Jack."

Along came Jack. Annie smiled. She had something in common with the former owner of this house. Jack's arrival, with Marcy, had been an unexpected godsend for her and for Savannah.

But now, along comes Sheldon Roth.

Less welcome than an F-4 twister in the middle of tornado alley.

Annie's smile faded, and she felt a shiver, like a sudden blast of cold wind on wet skin.

She returned to the main floor of the house and waited while Jack looked for a tool in the garage.

In a way, she told herself emphatically, it was good news that Peter—Sheldon—had reappeared now, as opposed to later. It was something like lancing a boil; she'd deal with it, get it over with, and never have to worry about him again. Sheldon Roth, living under a brand new name and unable to safely set foot in the United States, would be in South America, or the Cayman Islands, or wherever financial criminals go to bask in the sun and lick salt off their margaritas.

And Savannah would be safe with her mom. That was Priority One. Just get through Ugly Friday, and slide into home base. Break free once and for all of the spider web that held her back, that kept her watching life from a distance.

"Come see the dining room," Jack said. She followed him to a very large open space at the back of the central living area. He had no furniture in it yet.

"What did the owner model this after?" she asked. "Versailles?"

"I had the same thought when I first saw it. Marcy and I could buy a dining room suite to seat twenty, and hire a footman to serve, or we could bag it as a dining room and buy roller skates. Then I saw the kitchen, which is the size of, well, not a closet, but less than half as big as it should be."

He took her into the kitchen, which had a boxed-in feel, especially with the large appliances. The cook could open the refrigerator and the oven, but not at the same time.

The traffic pattern from the kitchen to the dining room was all wrong, too. Jack explained what he intended to do to open up the space, taking down one wall and part of another, co-opting one-third of the cavernous dining room into the new, spacious kitchen, and removing the low false ceiling to make the kitchen, dining room, and living room a unified space. The beautiful cedar ceiling would tie everything together.

"And the Florenz fireplace will go right here," he concluded. "The previous owner, as you must have guessed by now, had no interest in cooking. I have a picture in my mind of him passing a bucket of fried chicken to nineteen elegantly dressed guests."

Annie visualized the changes he'd described and easily—far too easily—imagined Savannah standing on a stepstool beside the proposed kitchen island.

The bedrooms were all upstairs. Jack followed her up a set of wide stairs with a gradual rise to a landing.

"Marcy's room, a small guest bedroom, and my home office will be on this floor. Come this way and I'll show you the master bedroom."

Another stairway angled off to the right, leading to an enormous bedroom, luxury bath and dressing area, plus a walk-in closet. The view from the bedroom showed that it was on the top of the hill. This was the cantilevered roof she'd seen when they drove up.

Everywhere she looked there were boxes. A few were open, and she saw linens inside, peach that matched the towels already in the bathroom.

As Jack outlined his plans for solar power and more subtle lighting for the hot tub outside French doors, he pulled sheets out of a box and made the bed.

"Somewhere here is a box marked 'Duvet and Pillows.'"

"Here it is." Annie pulled out a pillow and worked it into a pillowcase while he did the other pillow and fluffed the duvet. Everything on the king-sized bed was peach and ivory.

She glanced at her watch. The hour she'd agreed to was almost up, but she wished time would stop for another hour or so. Her cell phone, tucked in a pocket of her full skirt, rang.

"Hello?"

"Mommy, can I—I mean, may I sleep over at Mrs. Stefano's house? With Marcy?"

"Someday, I'm sure that will be fine."

"I mean tonight. Marcy's going to call Jack."

Annie would have reminded Savannah to call him Mr. Cabrini, but he'd insisted it was too formal for good friends.

Reasons to say "No" crowded Annie's mind, but she said, "I'll have to think about it. Please give the phone to Mrs. Stefano."

Jack's eyebrows went up. She moved the phone away from her face and said, "Savannah and Marcy are doing an end run around us. They want to stay with Vera tonight."

He held out his hand, and she gave him the phone. "Aunt Vera? Yes, hello. What are you up to?"

He listened a moment. "All *their* idea? Somehow, knowing you as I do, I doubt that. Put Marcy on, please." Another pause. "Marcy? What's up with this?"

He listened, nodded, listened some more. "Hold on." To Annie he said, "The invitation from Vera is legitimate. She has extra toothbrushes and T-shirts for nightgowns, and the three of them just started watching a DVD. I'm inclined to say yes, but it's up to you. We need to present a united front."

Annie hugged her arms close to her. She wanted to say no, but why?

Because if I don't have to pick up Savannah, I'll be alone here with Jack. With no compelling reason to leave. And one hell of a compelling reason to stay.

The look in his eyes left no room for doubt. He was thinking the same thing she was. And in case she needed a stronger hint, he pressed some buttons on a panel beside the door. With a soft whirring noise, cloth window blinds slid across the large windows and slowly rotated, cloaking the room in privacy. The full moon disappeared from sight. Another button and the lights dimmed.

She held out her hand for the phone. "Hello, Marcy. Would you please give the phone to Savannah?"

"Mommy, may I stay? Please?"

"If you promise to go to bed by ten o'clock—which is past your usual bedtime—you may stay."

Savannah agreed, but Annie made her say it out loud so Vera would know what deal had been struck.

"You're on your honor, girlfriend." Her words were drowned out by Savannah's chattering to Marcy. "Good night." She pressed End and smiled ruefully at Jack.

He wasted no time taking her in his arms. "Remind me to send flowers to Vera tomorrow," he murmured, then claimed her mouth.

For a long, exquisite moment, Annie surrendered, swept away by sensations she thought must be visible as electric arcs all over her body. Then she heard someone say, "Wait."

It took time for the message to reach her brain. She was the one who'd said, "Wait."

"Jack, wait," she said again, turning her lips away. Her knees had gone limp. Her whole body, in fact, was in danger of sliding to the floor. She held on tight with her arms around his neck.

"What's wrong?" He kissed a path down her cheek to her collarbone.

She released her hold on his neck and discovered she didn't have to keep herself upright. He held her against him from her breasts to her kneecaps.

"What's wrong?" she repeated. "Where do I begin?"

He tugged at the elastic at the neckline of her blouse and pulled it down, kissing lower and lower.

"I believe I'm developing a collarbone fetish," he said.

"I don't think you're listening to me."

"Sure I am. You're saying, 'Hold me tighter, kiss me again.' Your body articulates very clearly."

"I hardly know you, Jack. And by the way, I have terrible taste in men."

He grinned. "So, you're saying your attraction to me is a strike against me? I demand a second opinion."

Her second opinion was the same as her first. Jack Cabrini was climbing over and digging under the wall she'd built around herself after her last heartbreak. To prove it, he moved his hips against her, and she felt the unmistakable press of his arousal. Again he captured her mouth, and his tongue did whatever it wanted to do.

Taking a breath, he spoke again, "Annie, listen. You made one mistake. Give yourself a break."

"You don't understand." She pulled away, breathing hard.

"Understand what?"

"That I'm falling in love with you!" Tears sprang to her eyes, and she covered her mouth with her hand. "I don't want—" Her chest rose and fell as if she'd run a mile.

Jack stepped back, surprised by her shivering. He looked in the bathroom, couldn't find a box of tissues. Gave her a washcloth instead.

He wanted to smack himself upside the head with a two by four for rushing her. What kind of a jerk was he? She looked as if she might throw up.

On the occasions in Denver that he took a woman to bed, there was no doubt the lady wanted sex. Just because he didn't take any dates to his home didn't mean there was no opportunity. And he had a lot more sultry invitations to "come over to my place" than he'd acted on.

But Annie was different. Hell, *he* was different. Ever since he saw Denver in his rearview mirror, he felt as if he'd shed a dry, outgrown skin.

He moved a stack of jeans and shirts off an armchair. "Come on, have a seat." When she bent her knees and settled into the chair, he moved the matching chair in front of her and sat in it, knee to knee.

"I'm sorry," she said. "I didn't mean..."

The words drifted away; her eyes looked anywhere but at him. He recognized that she probably wasn't going to say again that she was falling in love with him. In fact, she'd probably pay dearly to retrieve those words. But once spoken, the word "love" hung in the air like perfume.

"No," he said at last. "I'm the one who's sorry. I showed the romantic finesse of Pavlov's dogs at mealtime."

She wrung her hands together and sucked up air in great gulps, trying not to cry. "You're not doing anything I don't want. I feel like a...like a committee. My body and mind take a vote—and then they demand a recount."

"Your mind isn't ready to go where your body wants to go," he said. "But that doesn't mean your body is wrong. Annie, give me a chance. I promise not to rush you." He tipped her chin up with his finger so she had to look him in the eye. "That promise doesn't mean I'm not aching to hold you."

"That's romantic." She smiled and wiped her cheeks, sniffling. "You've probably figured out by now I'm a sucker for romance. The kind of sucker with a hard shell and a soft center."

"I'll file that information away for future reference."

"I've spent six years hardening my shell and shrinking my center."

"He hurt you a lot."

"I was such a fool. I'd never been close to falling in love and getting married before I met Peter. I expected falling in love would be like settling onto a down comforter. But it was more like...falling out of an airplane. First my main parachute failed. Then my reserve chute failed."

"So feeling attracted to me increases your fear."

She searched his face for any sign of humor, but instead she saw kindness. Concern. Sincerity. She swallowed hard and nodded.

"It's a stronger response than fight or flight," she explained. "I get anxiety attacks. Heart palpitations, cold sweat, pain in my chest, the works. Medication helps."

"Do you have any with you?"

"No. But I'm feeling better now. I'll be all right."

"Do you want me to take you home? You call the shots."

Do I want...? Do I? Pros and cons battled in her head like screaming baseball coaches. The job of umpire wore her out, but Jack was right. She had to call the shots.

He said he wouldn't rush me. She took a deep breath, exhaled slowly, and met his cool, collected, and unwavering gaze with one of her own.

And then...Jack Cabrini smiled. And Annie Riker could swear she heard the sound of her hard shell cracking. She had to wet her lips to say anything at all.

"I want to stay."

Chapter Eleven

"Here we are by the altar," Jack said. His dad and Beatrice beamed at the photographer, ecstatically happy, and Vera looked glad to be there. Jack, however, looked like a man whose sandpaper underwear was riding up in the crotch.

Annie had tucked her bare feet under her on the dark red leather couch. "He doesn't look old enough to be your father. I mean, he does, but there's something so young in his face, too. Maybe that's what being in love does for people."

Jack took the framed photo back and studied it. Reaching into the open box of carefully wrapped photos, professional diplomas, and plaques, he pulled out a photo of his dad and mom on their wedding day.

"Oh, my gosh," Annie said. "Flower children?"

"I know. I can't believe it myself." Ace had an enormous drooping mustache and long, wiry hair. The shirttail of his white African-style shirt—what did they call it? A dashiki?—hung down over his striped, bell-bottom pants. His bride, Jack's mom, wore a long skirt made of white cotton and a tie-died flowing tunic. Her long, straight hair was crowned with flowers, and a lei dangled from her neck.

"She was beautiful. Your dad looks older here than he did twenty-some years later. Well, maybe older isn't the right word. More serious."

"More scared. He told me he felt like he was jumping off a cliff. They were still in college and had no money. They drove a Gremlin. Frog green."

"You're lucky they didn't name you Icarus or Moonshadow. The people behind them look like they're auditioning for *Hair*. Where was this taken?"

"Boulder. I believe the moon was in the seventh house, and Jupiter aligned with Mars."

Looking at the mom he'd lost at age eleven, and the dad he'd turned his back on as a man, made his heart pinch.

His mom, Julie, never lost her zest for life.

Jack had seen a lot of people get seriously, some even terminally, ill and *then* discover that life was a treasure. Julie Cabrini treasured life long before she got sick.

Instead of treating her son like a little simpleton, sugar-coating her cancer diagnosis—or lying about it as so many people do—she met cancer face-on, and she expected him to do the same.

He put the photos away and added wood to the gleaming stove.

"I'll be right back." In the kitchen, he unpacked one of the padded boxes of wine he'd brought to Montana in his truck, selected a bottle of pinot grigio, and removed the cork.

He took a look at his cell phone, which had vibrated in his pocket three times now. He certainly hoped it was something that could wait. He and Annie needed time alone to get better acquainted.

With a sigh, he pressed Travis's name on his speed dial. Three calls could not be ignored. And it might be good news. Maybe the D.A. had made a deal with the Queen of Darkness and her minions.

"Jack," Travis answered with no *Hello.* "I talked to the district attorney and his deputy. Their case is disintegrating. Cruella has paid the witnesses to shut up, and the former secretary of the interior won't let his son testify unless Marcy testifies."

"Then I guess it's over, because I'm not dragging Marcy into that pest hole."

"Jack...we can't discuss this on the phone like it's a tee time. I'll be in Bitter Falls tomorrow."

"Listen to me, Travis," Jack barked, but he was

talking to himself. He redialed Travis's number and got voicemail. He swore under his breath. Travis was wasting jet fuel coming to Montana, but there was nothing Jack could do to stop him.

He put it out of his mind—since he had no choice—and returned to Annie, the open wine bottle in one hand and two crystal wine glasses dangling in the other.

She took the glasses; he poured the wine and watched her taste it.

"Thanks. This is good." She held up her glass and touched it to his. "Your health."

"And yours." With a remote control, he turned off the lights in the central living room where they sat. They had enough light from the fireplace and the recessed lighting in the reading nook.

"I didn't notice until now," he said, "but the raised section of the living room looks like a stage. Especially when it's lit this way."

"You could stage *Our Town*. I played Emily in high school." She clasped her hands against her chest, dramatically, and proclaimed, "'Oh, earth, you're too wonderful for anybody to realize you. Do any human beings ever realize life while they live it? Every, every minute?'"

She sighed and held out her hands, palms up, as if to say, *Silly, huh? Don't mind me.*

He was pretty sure she was blushing, which only made her prettier. The firelight danced in her blue eyes.

"Somewhere in this mess," he gestured at the stacks of boxes they'd had to weave through to get to the couch, "I have a complete set of Thornton Wilder's works."

Annie was close enough that he could lean forward and touch her shoulder with his outstretched hand, but he kept his hands to himself. He was determined to give her all the space she needed. Or, rather, that she thought she needed.

What she *really* needed, he was certain, was to be in his arms.

He leaned his back against one large rolled arm of the couch and stretched his feet, crossed at the ankles, out on the floor, close by the couch.

"I'm ready to hear all about your grandmother Goldie," he said. "How many greats?"

"Great-great-grandmother." She gave him the rundown, focusing on the enmity between Goldie and her son's wife, Greta, and how it carried forward to block her mom, Diana, from ever knowing who her birth parents were.

"Sounds like Goldie reaped what she sowed," he observed.

Annie nodded and sipped her wine. "Goldie's stubbornness kept her alive and brought her out of the Klondike with a fortune, but it was her worst flaw. Probably the civil war in the Jones family started as simple jealousy. Lord knows Goldie wasn't the first or last woman to resent a daughter-in-law. Jealousy, compounded by stubbornness."

She sipped her wine and stared at the dancing flames behind the treated glass. "But the concrete hardened when Greta's second son died. There's no way to say whether Goldie's money and the doctors Stanley and Greta could have paid would have saved the baby, but Greta always believed it could have."

"Woulda, coulda, shoulda," he said softly. He thought of Goldie, and Greta, and of Marcy's mom, Beatrice...and of slick Sheldon Roth. Swindling a fortune from investors, and breaking the heart of Annie Riker. Crushing her trust under his heel with no more thought than a bum grinding out a cigarette butt.

"Family is a funny thing," she said.

"I was thinking the same thing."

She unfolded her legs and set her wineglass on an unopened cardboard box. On her knees, she crept closer to him and lay down. Her hips were beside his, angled toward him, and her head reached his shoulder.

He rolled onto his left hip and pulled his feet onto the couch. He'd bought it because it was designed for tall people, the seat a little higher than the average, and quite a bit deeper front to back. It was perfect, he now discovered, for full body cuddling.

"That sound you hear," he murmured, "is contentment."

Actually, he thought as he pulled her up a few inches so he could claim her mouth, it was the sound of his DNA purring. If he were an elk, he'd be bugling.

She slid her left foot up and down his right leg. He groaned and deepened the kiss.

He gained sudden respect for the cliché, *Where have you been all my life?* And he knew—for the first time—why "fall" was the right verb for love.

Her left hand was under his T-shirt, scratching playfully at his back, then moving to his chest and tracing his muscles. He gasped, breaking the kiss.

"I've wanted to do that since the first moment I saw you," she said.

With one hand he pulled the shirt over his head and threw it across the room. "Anything else you have a mind to explore?"

"Now that you mention it," she murmured. As she opened her mouth to another kiss, she cupped his butt and squeezed his thigh through his jeans.

He clutched her close and rotated so she was on top of him.

"It's a waste to have one of your hands pinned underneath you."

She laughed and kneaded the muscles of his chest. "So much of you, so little time."

"Don't fret about the time. I just need to be at work in the morning. And you already told Tess that you're with me, and Savannah is with Vera overnight. Your sister can probably add one and one."

He lunged up and kissed her, making her laugh.

"There's something else I've been wanting to do," she said.

He loved the husky sound of her voice. "Surprise me."

She wiggled her hips to move down, and the pressure against his erection, even through her skirt and his jeans, made him blurt, "Oh, my God."

"You, sir, are very easily surprised." She lowered her face to his chest and traced lazy circles around his nipples.

Making a humming noise that might be the start of a laugh, or maybe the sound a tigress makes before she takes the first bite, Annie flicked her tongue across one nipple, then the other one.

He grabbed fistfuls of her skirt in both hands, pulled it up, and plunged both hands into her tight silk panties and fondled her butt. He was panting like he'd run a race.

"You're not the only one with fantasies," he said, one hand on her butt and the other on its way to her breast. It was all he could do to form words into a sentence. "I need more hands."

She began shaking with laughter. The rocking movement drove him even crazier.

Suddenly she stopped laughing, but she kept moving her hips up and down. "Oh, Jack, that feels so good."

Again he made a quick change of position, kneeling beside the couch and rolling Annie onto her back. It took only a moment to find the zipper on the skirt and slide it down her legs. He hooked his fingers in her panties and moved them down a few inches, but her hand stopped his.

"Jack, I know we're way out in the country, but I feel like I'm in a fishbowl. Would you—?"

He groped on the floor to find the remote control

and turned off the lights in the reading nook. Now the only light was the faint glow of coals in the freestanding fireplace.

"Better?" he asked.

"Yes. Thanks." She sat up enough to remove her blouse.

The sight of her in only her bra and panties made his jeans two sizes too small. He undid the metal button and felt the zipper slide down of its own accord. There must have been a time he'd been this turned on, but he'd be damned if he could remember it.

He slid his left arm under her shoulders and felt her curl against him. "So beautiful," he murmured, bending to kiss the high mounds of her perfect breasts, exploring the valley with his tongue and dipping it below the lacy edge of each cup.

As if eager for more, Annie released the tiny plastic clasp beneath her breasts and let it fall open. With a touch as light as a whisper, he pulled the cups away.

The taste of her hard nipples was exquisite. He kissed down her belly and easily tugged her panties down. She tossed them aside with a flick of her toes.

He grinned. "Mmmmm, mmmm, mmmm." This time the tiger instead of the tigress. "So much of you, so little time."

As he claimed her mouth again and she plunged her tongue into his, her right hand closed around the shaft of his erection. Even through his briefs, the pressure almost sent him into shock. He swore softly, and she chuckled.

"You have on too many clothes."

"Not for long!" He stood. Taking a moment to get a foil packet out of his back pocket, he dropped his jeans and briefs.

She edged to the back of the couch, lying on her right side, and patted the leather beside her. As soon as he lay beside her, facing her, she stroked his erection again and cupped him. Her hot hand worked the moisture at the tip down the shaft. To show him what she wanted, she did that fantastic toes-on-leg rub again.

Part of his brain said he should take his time, but the lady was saying something else entirely. "Jack, I want you."

Quickly, he sheathed himself and slipped inside her. A few slow strokes, deeper, breathing hard, harder. The sound of her moaning, her mouth beneath his.

Unexpectedly, she gripped him tight with both arms, and he felt the convulsions of her climax.

"Jack, Jack."

Two more strokes and he was over the top with her, over the top and soaring.

Annie buried her face against Jack's chest. The voice in her head that had babbled incessantly since he'd taken her in his arms, tonight, in his bedroom...that voice was finally too shocked to berate her. All the nagging, provocative questions evaporated into the darkened room.

What will he think of me? What will I think of myself?

What if I reach over and brazenly cup him? What if I don't?

What if we make love once, and then—he's not interested in me?

Those questions were drowned out by one other.

What if I died without knowing what it felt like to make love with Jack?

Woulda. Coulda. Shoulda.

Her expectations had been outrageously high. But the real thing had been so much better.

As her breathing calmed, she traced the cut of the muscles in his arm, letting her fingers wander to his chest and to his cheek. Before the voice could take over her mind, sifting every word she might say, looking for errors, and sifting every word Jack might say, searching for hidden meanings, she spoke from her heart.

"Jack, that was the best I ever—I mean, it was, ummm, for me it was the best."

He pressed her head against his shoulder and kissed her forehead. His right hand rested on her hip; her left leg was draped over his thigh. He stroked her hip and her leg.

"I feel like..." His voice drifted away. She wondered if he'd dozed off. She was sleepy, too.

He spoke again. "A poem is going around in my mind."

She turned her ear to his chest wall and listened to his heart beat. She knew, deep inside herself, that what Jack was about to say was more intimate, more risky for him to share, than sex. "Tell me."

"The Chambered Nautilus."

She smiled and kissed the palm of his hand. "'Build thee more stately mansions, O my soul.' Oliver Wendell Holmes."

"You know it, huh?" He chuckled, and she heard the rumble in his chest. "I guess it's the best poem for an architect to know."

"True. But I can tell it means more to you than a blueprint for a larger edifice."

She rested her chin on her hand and watched his face. Jack was a construction C.E.O., the guy who put in sewer lines, and power cables, and sump pumps. A jackhammer and backhoe guy. But he was an architect, too. An artist. A stack-of-good-books in the winter guy.

"Tell me," she said softly. "More stately mansions."

She waited in the comfortable silence, reciting what she recalled of the poem in her mind. It was about a tropical mollusk that started out in a tiny shell. As it grew, it secreted pearl-like material to add on to its shell, each curved compartment added onto the one before in a spreading spiral. As soon as its new home was ready, it moved forward, tentacles and all, and sealed off the space behind it.

"'Leave thy low-vaulted past!'" Jack quoted. "Well, I'm making changes professionally, and personally—where it concerns being available like I should be, for Marcy—but there's a whole other part of life that I've avoided. The notion of true intimacy scares the pants off me."

He laughed. "No, that's not true. I usually keep my pants on and get home in time for Jay Leno. Anyway, my point is, with you, I'm all in. Heart and mind as well as body."

Tears welled in her eyes. She couldn't say a word.

"Annie, I won't hold you to what you said about falling in love with me, not yet. But I'm not going anywhere, so if you're falling, I'm ready to catch you."

She put both hands on his shoulders and pulled herself up so they were face to face. She studied the firm jaw and warm eyes; she ran her fingers through his hair. She was falling, all right. Cartwheeling through space. And yet this fall didn't frighten her. Instead, she was exhilarated.

From the heap of clothes on the floor she heard her cell phone. "I'd better get that," she said with real regret. Leaning over his chest, she snagged her skirt and dragged it toward her.

As she searched for the pocket, she added, "Savannah has never spent the night without either me or Tess."

She pulled out the ringing phone and pressed Talk quickly so it wouldn't go to voicemail. "Hello?"

"Annie?" A woman's voice. Tense.

"Yes?" She pushed herself to her knees.

"This is Delia Phinney."

"What-?" She didn't like the sound of Delia's voice. Something was wrong. "What is it, Delia?" To Jack she mouthed the words, *my lawyer.*

"Don't come to Seattle, Annie."

"Don't come to Seattle? What's going on?"

"There won't be a meeting with Sheldon Roth. There won't be any meeting at his lawyer's office."

Annie felt nausea rise and walked backward on her knees, away from Jack.

He sat up and whispered, "What's wrong?"

"No meeting," she said woodenly into the phone. To Jack she said, without moving the phone, "Something happened in Seattle. Delia, what happened?"

When she answered, Annie crumpled like a rag doll. "Tonight?" was all she could say. She listened, then shook her head, *No. No.* "Delia, I'll call you back in a few minutes."

She snapped the phone shut and hugged her arms around herself. Only one minute ago she'd reveled in lying naked. Now she wanted layers and layers of clothing. She wanted to race out of Jack's house, grab her daughter and race out of Montana.

"Annie," Jack said, "tell me what's wrong."

She exhaled. "Someone, apparently a professional hit man, burst into the home of Sheldon's attorney. About four hours ago. Sheldon was there. The gunman shot and killed the attorney, tried to shoot Sheldon, but he got away. He took his attorney's car. Nobody knows where he is."

"And the gunman?"

"He got away. He ripped a handful of pages out of the file that was open on the lawyer's desk. Presumably, he's hot on Sheldon's trail."

Jack folded her in his arms, and she gave in to the shakes that wracked her body.

"Let's get dressed," he said. "I'll put some coffee on while you get ready to call her back."

"What if he—?" She clutched Jack's arm as he stood to go toward the kitchen. "What if Sheldon comes here?"

"He's probably out of the country already."

"But, what—" She swallowed hard. "What if the gunman comes to take Savannah?" She knew her voice was rising; she knew she was digging her fingernails into Jack's skin. She didn't care. Hysteria made her heart pound as if it would explode from her chest. She began hyperventilating, and her chest hurt.

"What if he thinks Sheldon will trade what he has for the life of his little girl?" A high keening noise came out of her.

Jack pulled her gently to her feet and wrapped his arms around her like a down comforter.

"It's going to be all right. We'll get through it."

"Oh, Jack." Her teeth chattered. "Jack, I'm so scared."

Chapter Twelve

The employee of the regional airline posted the new time for the flight to Missoula. Another two hours on top of the hour and a half they'd already waited.

"Oh, crap," Mike Hale said. "At this rate it'll be dawn before we're airborne. You want more coffee?"

"No, thanks. I'm going to try to sleep."

Waiting at the gate at Seattle-Tacoma International Airport, Deputy U.S. Marshal Susan Hightower closed her eyes, but sleep evaded her. Instead, she went over—and over—the events of the past six hours.

It had started after dinner when she and Mike had heard, on their scanner, that gunshots were heard at the home of Isaac Chenoweth. A Hummer, with a man at the wheel, had rocketed through the garage door. Another man, with a gun, was seen running out of the garage. He'd sprinted up the street and left in a "small black car."

They'd gone back to headquarters, where they learned nothing for nearly an hour, then heard that the damaged Hummer had been found, abandoned, on the ferry to Bremerton.

Not long after that, Susan had lost what was left of her temper.

In the conference room where she'd admired the view the previous afternoon, she'd waited for a briefing to start, only to find it had been canceled and fellow marshal Tony Alberghetti was there to toss an assignment to Susan and Mike. He had the smarmy look of a teacher's pet left in charge of the classroom while the teacher took a break.

Susan had shot to her feet with the agility of a cougar and pressed one stiff finger into the breastbone of Tony Al. He'd pushed her too far this time, and she was damn sure going to push back.

"I don't care who you know, Tony. You're not in the FBI yet, so don't do their dirty work. I'm in this case to solve it. To catch the fugitive. So don't you dare tell anyone the Marshals Service stands ready to 'support' them."

"Did anyone ever tell you you're cute when you're mad?" He pressed forward until their faces were six inches apart. "No? I know why."

"I haven't been called cute since I was three years old and signed up for karate lessons instead of tap dance."

"Okay, okay," he said, backing up. "Don't be such a damn ball buster, will you? You and Mike can get over to the ferry. Coordinate, you know the drill. They're towing the Hummer off at Bremerton."

"The FBI can handle that chore. *Coordinate, you know the drill.*" She sliced the words like a Ginzu knife. "And FBI Special Agents are universally loved by all local cops. Let's go, Mike."

"Where are you going?" Tony yelled.

Mike was close on her heels. Rather than wait for the elevator and risk running into C. Edgar Sommers, they took the stairs. In the lobby, they reentered the secure area by running their badges through a scanner and hurried down a long hall toward the parking garage.

"I'll drive," Mike said.

"Chicken," she muttered, sliding into the driver's seat before he could. "I'm not crazy. I'm focused."

"I gather from what you said that we're not going to the ferry?"

"No! There's a reason that Tony Al and the FBI want us to process the Hummer. Because it's a dead end. We might as well wrap ourselves in red tape and order in breakfast, because once we sign in, we'll never get out of there."

"We're going to the lawyer's house?"

"Of course." As soon as she'd cleared the parking garage ramp, she hit the button for lights and siren.

Mike read the address off the dashboard computer. She headed for the west side of Mercer Island, the expensive, forested enclave in the middle of Lake Washington. Interstate 90 spanned the island by surface road and two tunnels.

Ten minutes later they drove slowly past the front of the mansion of Isaac Chenoweth, Attorney-at-law; partner in a law firm with six names, two of them Chenoweth.

Now the home of a dead man.

They parked down the street and walked back. When they'd signed into the scene, they entered the mansion, put paper booties over their boots, and tried to get close enough to look at the body.

Susan looked around the extravagantly appointed foyer and up the curving stairway.

"I think I've seen this place before. In *Gone with the Wind*. It just goes to prove the old saying. You can't take it with you."

FBI Special Agent Cletus Rohatyn walked out of the dining room and caught sight of them.

"Aren't you supposed to be on your way to Bremerton?"

"To do what?" Susan said, her voice cold with menace. "Handle the insurance claim on the Hummer? I. Don't. Think. So."

"Well, you're in the fugitive chasing business. And he's. Not. Here."

"He's not in Bremerton, either," she said with a smile. "Betcha ten dead presidents."

"Which dead president?" Rohatyn said. "Washington?"

"Andrew Jackson."

"Oooo. Big bettor, huh?" He barked a laugh.

"You're on. Now go to Bremerton and prove it."

"Nope. I learned in law school that I can't prove a negative. I'm going to find out where Sheldon Roth is, not where he isn't."

Someone called Rohatyn to the phone, and Susan moved quickly into a space that had opened to allow the medical examiner to exit. He told an assistant to pack the body for transit.

At the far side of an enormous hardwood desk, still in a throne-sized chair, slumped the body of Isaac Chenoweth. The front of his yellow shirt was drenched with blood, and the papers on the desk were all red and wet.

Isaac Chenoweth, Esquire, wouldn't be objecting to any remarks from the prosecution, nor would he be addressing the ladies and gentlemen of the jury.

Susan had seen him work, and he was a sly, fearless, conniving bastard, totally without scruples. If she'd ever been arrested, he was the lawyer she would have hired.

Listening intently as the homicide detectives answered the questions of the medical examiner, she picked up valuable facts. Isaac Chenoweth had been meeting with his client, Sheldon Roth, newly released from federal prison, in his home office with its spectacular view of Lake Washington and, to the west, the skyline of Seattle. A man broke in through French doors from the patio and enclosed lap pool beyond it. He shot Chenoweth before he had time to even think about running, then fired at least four more shots. From the location of the bullet holes, he'd been on his way out of the room, heading toward the kitchen.

Crime techs were removing bullets from the hallway and dusting the door to the garage for fingerprints.

A nanny-cam had been running from a bookshelf filled with expensive Native American pottery, the camera hidden inside a fake Hopi Kachina doll. The digital photo chip, no sound recorded, was taken as evidence by Bellevue P.D., and the FBI agents were furious.

Rohatyn was on the phone about it, and his face was red with rage. Susan guessed from the smile on the face of a plainclothes detective, Bellevue P.D., that he'd made that decision. He held the power in the room.

She backed up, went around the corner into a living room the size of a tennis court and imagined the realtor's spiel about how perfect it was for entertaining.

Such as a reception following a funeral.

A woman about fifty years old sat on a couch against the farthest wall in the room. From the expensive clothes she wore and the wads of tissue all over the couch, Susan guessed she was the widow.

She whispered to Mike to keep listening to the turf war and to get the name and phone numbers for the lead detective. "I'm going to talk to her." She gestured with her chin.

"Hello, ma'am." She identified herself and pulled an ottoman of soft ivory leather in front of her. "Are you Mrs. Chenoweth?"

She nodded. "My husband was murdered in cold blood."

"Were you in the house? Did you hear the gunshots?"

"I told the detective everything I know."

"I understand, it's horrible for you to go over it again and again. But I'm trying to find Sheldon Roth, and you might be able to help me."

"He stole our car, our Hummer. He just backed it right out of the garage and ripped the garage door off."

"Was he trying to get away from the man with the gun? I think that's what I heard them say."

"I don't know. I heard the shots. I was upstairs in my bedroom, trying on these new boots. I knew right away it was a gun. I locked my bedroom door and went in my bathroom and locked that door, too. Then I called nine-one-one. That's what my husband always told me to do."

"He was absolutely right. So you saw nothing?"

"Yes. I mean, no. After I locked the bedroom door, I looked out the window and saw our Hummer smash out through the door. It was a horrible noise."

"And you think Sheldon Roth was driving?"

"I'm sure of it. I'd spoken with him before I went upstairs. It was him. I saw him by the floodlight in front of the garage. Then I ran into the bathroom. I stayed on the phone with the nine-one-one operator until a policeman came and identified himself. Then I unlocked the door."

Susan heard a loud argument at the front door.

"That's my daughter, Edie," Mrs. Chenoweth said. "Go tell that obnoxious man at the door that I want my daughter with me. Who the hell does he think he is, anyway?"

"Who, indeed?" Susan said, adopting Mrs. C's indignation.

At the door she faced a spectacular brunette, six feet tall, wearing clothes that might as well have been knit from U.S. Currency. "Edie," she said, "thank goodness you're here. You signed in with the officer by the street?"

"Of course I did."

"Your mother's in here. Come with me."

The officer at the door shrugged. No skin off his nose.

As they crossed the room, a process slowed by sinking into the carpet at every step, Susan introduced herself.

"Edie Chenoweth," the brunette responded by habit.

Susan watched the mother-and-child reunion impatiently, finally asking them to forgive her for interrupting, but she had to ask a couple questions.

The answers were worth the wait. Edie Chenoweth, also an attorney and a junior partner in the firm, had assisted her father at every juncture of the Sheldon Roth matter.

Susan tip-toed around the "Roth matter," trying not to ask questions that would get No for an answer, or worse, earn Edie's hostility.

It was clear, quickly, that Sheldon Roth had charmed the pants off Edie Chenoweth, whether figuratively or literally Susan didn't know. But Edie feared for Sheldon's safety and believed that he needed protection.

Thinking quickly, Susan convinced her that the U.S. Marshals Service, not the FBI, was the agency to trust.

"Whoever shot your father tried to kill Sheldon, too."

Edie, who sat on the couch holding her crying mother against her, said her father had brought home a folder she'd prepared. It had Sheldon's new passport, five thousand dollars cash, and some other documents, things they had to take care of before he left the country.

"Relinquishment?" Susan asked. "Parental rights?"

Edie shook her head no, then changed her mind. "That was on top. Dad had to change a few words."

Susan walked toward the entryway and saw the body bag getting wheeled out. The detective she'd seen earlier stood in the library, shoulders hunched over. Suddenly he turned on his heel and strode into the entryway, past Susan, and into the living room.

As she watched, he helped Edie to her feet and, touching her elbow, walked her to the door of the room.

"A folder is open on the desk," he said softly. "Some pages have been ripped out, possibly by Sheldon Roth, possibly by the person who shot your father. I'm going to carry it over here and show you.

I'm hoping you can tell us what was taken. I have to warn you, Ms. Chenoweth, the pages have blood on them."

She swallowed hard and nodded. "Go ahead."

Susan watched him lift the open folder and, with gloved hands, carry it to Edie. A look passed between Edie and Susan.

Edie swallowed hard and stared at the bloody pages. Finally she nodded. "It was a list of questions, five pages long, that the FBI wanted answered before Mr. Roth could leave Seattle. There could have been something else. I have a duplicate file in the safe at our office. I don't want to leave my mother right now, though. Let me take her to a hotel and get my younger sister to stay with her. Then I'll go to the office."

Susan returned to Mrs. Chenoweth's side, waiting for Edie. As the two of them got the older woman to her feet, Susan asked her question.

"Was the relinquishment document gone?"

Edie nodded.

"Did it have Annie Riker's address?"

Edie froze. Looked up suddenly. Nodded.

Susan gave her a card and asked for Edie's. Wrote down Edie's personal cell phone number on the back.

"I'll be in touch. Thanks for your help."

Outside, she caught Mike's eye and gestured. *Let's go.*

In the car, in the passenger seat, she turned her cell phone back on. Delia Phinney had called.

"This will be unpleasant," she said as Mike wove around the crime scene truck and onto the road. "Sheldon Roth, with a new passport and cash, is probably out of the country by now, or, at least, on a plane headed out of the country. That would be the conventional wisdom."

"I think I hear a *However* coming," Mike said.

Susan sighed. "However, I have to tell Ms.

Phinney I have a hinky feeling."

"What's that?" Mike asked. "You were with the lawyer's wife and daughter quite a while. You must have figured something out."

"I have a hunch that Sheldon Roth is on his way to Montana."

She thought about the pages ripped from the folder. They didn't have information Sheldon needed; he already knew what they said. And, if he'd hung around after Chenoweth's upper body landed on the file, he would have been shot, not missed on his way out of the room as the bullet holes showed. Only the shooter had time to lift Chenoweth's torso and tear pages from the open file.

She cleared her throat and prepared to click on Delia Phinney's phone number.

"And the other half of my hunch is that a hit man could be following him to Annie Riker's address."

****

"Susan? They're calling our flight. Let's go."

"You drive," she mumbled. "I'm too sleepy."

Mike laughed. "This time I think I'll let a professional drive. Come on. You can go back to sleep in a few minutes."

Chapter Thirteen

Jack looked at his watch. Half-past midnight.

"Have a seat, please," the young officer, whose uniform nametag read Ramm, said. "Deputy Pacheco will be with you in a couple minutes. Would you like some coffee?"

"No, thanks," Jack answered.

The officer pressed numbers on a keypad beside a metal door. When it buzzed, he went through; the door made a loud *clank* as it shut.

To their right was the information window, probably bulletproof glass, where they'd asked to speak to the sheriff. The young woman in the cubicle, also in uniform, had pushed a button and called, "Deputy Ramm to the lobby, please."

Jack stared at the door through which the young deputy had disappeared. More coffee was the last thing he needed right now. He and Annie had each drunk two cups of French roast while they got dressed, and while they talked to Delia Phinney.

Before they came to the Silver County Sheriff's Department, they'd gone to Annie's house so she could change to jeans and take the medicine she needed to relieve anxiety attacks.

"It doesn't make me sleepy," she'd told him. "It does something to soothe the panic part of the brain. Some people take it in order to get past their fear of flying, or terror of medical procedures."

Instead of calling Delia back on her cell phone, Annie had used the two portable phones in Jack's house. She wanted him to be on another line so she wouldn't miss important information.

"The FBI has the lead on this," Delia told them,

"but I've been in touch with Deputy U. S. Marshal Susan Hightower. You said yesterday that you remember her."

"Yes." Annie's head bobbed up and down.

"I found out from the United States Attorney's office," Delia continued, "that although technically Sheldon was out of prison, he wasn't free to go until he'd given a deposition on 'Big.' That's somebody's code name for the head of a West Coast criminal enterprise."

Jack had rolled his eyes. Someone in a position of power was a fan of *Sex and the City*.

"I don't know who it is," Delia had told them. "I did manage to squeeze out that the federal judge who suddenly retired and disappeared is probably playing some part in this. And, yes, he's the judge who sentenced Sheldon Roth. Walter Sommers. His brother, C. Edgar, is the Seattle bureau chief of the Marshals Service."

Jack observed that the lobby's lights were dim, a good idea to save energy in the middle of the night. He rose and crossed the room to examine a wall display of police shields; he returned to his seat. Took Annie's hand in his.

She was calmer since she'd taken the medication, but the skin on her hands was still raw where she'd been wringing them.

"A couple things don't automatically add up," she said.

"Yes?"

"Judge Sommers retired suddenly and dropped out of sight. My first thought was that he's involved in a negative way. But maybe he's on the right side and has to be protected."

"Good point. What else?"

"I don't think very many people knew where Sheldon would be tonight. The FBI might have a leak. Or Chenoweth's office. In fact," she added, getting animated, "maybe the shooting had nothing to do with Sheldon. Chenoweth probably has a hundred enemies. Maybe the guy simply tried to shoot the witness."

Jack said nothing.

"Unlikely, at best," she said with a sigh. "Sheldon Roth has a lot of enemies."

The door opened, and Deputy Ramm leaned out. "Come with me, please, sir, ma'am."

Down a hallway, past three cubicles with desktop computers but empty of people at this hour, the officer stood aside by an open door. Jack and Annie entered and shook hands with Deputy Sheriff Pauline Pacheco.

"Please, have a seat. What can I do for you?"

Jack listened to Annie explain her fear that federal fugitive Sheldon Roth would come to Bitter Falls. She wasn't afraid of Roth, she said, who had never been accused of any violent crime. His criminality was strictly white collar. Massive swindling and money laundering.

"And bigamy," she added, "although the jury found him not guilty on that."

Annie ran her fingers through her hair and looked from Jack to Deputy Pacheco. A wave of nausea passed through her, and she paused to catch her breath. The jury—and Annie herself—had watched Sheldon's defense lawyer destroy "Mr. Roth's so-called second wife" on the stand. Clearly fragile, the woman had backed away from every fact that was on her side. By the time Isaac Chenoweth was finished with her, she would have admitted to shooting Abraham Lincoln.

Annie had refused to testify; that was why she was in the courtroom to witness the debacle. She wanted to march forward, to tell the jury that the woman was telling the truth, but it was too late.

She'd had her chance to do the right thing, and she'd refused. The public humiliation would have ruined her life, and it would have followed her innocent unborn child. She'd had to refuse. Hadn't she?

"To him," she added, "bigamy wasn't a crime. He's such a narcissist that he thinks he was doing us a favor. A piece of Sheldon Roth, by his reasoning, was better than none of him."

Pacheco asked about Savannah. Did Sheldon know he had a daughter?

"Biologically, yes. I found out I was pregnant before he was arrested, when I was still under the delusion that I was a married woman."

Nausea rocked her again. A memory as clear as High-Def TV.

Me, checking the pregnancy test strip. Me, grabbing the phone to call the man I'd married six weeks earlier.

"Peter! You're going to be a daddy!"

Annie explained how his only interest in Savannah was as a tool to control people. "Especially to control me. After he went to prison, I tried to get him to sign a document relinquishing parental rights. All this time he's refused to do so. When he got out of prison, about two days ago, he used 'signing the document' as a way to get me to Seattle. He's like a puppeteer. He likes to make people dance."

"Why is it important to you to get such a document signed?" Pacheco asked. "If he has no interest in her, why does it matter what he signs?"

"My first concern is to ensure that Savannah can never, ever be taken away from me. Believe me, Deputy Pacheco, I've never believed Sheldon Roth would stay in prison for a long time. And he would try to take Savannah just to prove he can do anything he wants. Second, if anything ever happens to me, Savannah must be adopted by my sister, Tess Riker. I've seen horrible things happen with people fighting over children. Naming Tess as my daughter's guardian, in my will, isn't enough."

"Two good reasons," Pacheco said.

"And now there's a third," Annie said. "My sister and I inherited property and cash worth many millions of dollars. I was only an amusement to Sheldon Roth—whom I knew as Peter Dylan—before. That I got pregnant was mildly interesting to him. That's all. But with this inheritance, his potential claim on my daughter terrifies me."

Annie was too overwrought to continue. The deputy gave her a bottle of water from a shelf near her desk.

Jack continued the story, relaying the details of the shooting at the Seattle attorney's house.

"What has Annie so scared," he said, "is that Sheldon's file was open on Isaac Chenoweth's desk. The lawyer's wife heard the shooting, and from upstairs she saw their Hummer, with Sheldon at the wheel, crash out through the garage door. The blood-soaked file had several pages ripped out, apparently by the gunman. The top sheet had Annie's information."

"The meeting where Sheldon would see my daughter, and then sign the relinquishment document, was set for Friday."

"Other files taken," Jack added, "had questions from the FBI. They probably had information about people he was discussing with the FBI."

"So, as those individuals would put it," Pacheco said, "it had information on the people he was 'ratting out.' People who would be infinitely grateful if he died with his mouth shut. A suspect-rich environment."

"I think you have it nailed," Jack said.

Pacheco summoned Officer Ramm and directed him to get patrol cars watching Annie's home, Vera's home, and to make periodic sweeps of Albion House. Then she picked up her phone and made some calls to the Bellevue Police Department's Homicide Division, the F.B.I., and to the U.S. Marshals

Service.

Forty minutes later they knew that two deputy United States marshals were on their way by plane to Missoula and would drive to Bitter Falls. Airlines were being checked for any sign of Sheldon Roth. It was the unanimous opinion of everyone she talked to that he was on a plane, traveling under a new alias, heading out of the country.

"Don't believe what you see on CSI," Pacheco told them. "He could have gone anywhere. I agree with you, sir. He probably wants to get out of the country. And, according to what your attorney said, Ms. Riker, he probably had a passport and cash."

Pacheco stood. "We've done everything we can for now. You folks need to get some rest. You won't be doing yourself or your daughter any favors by falling asleep on your feet. I've left my number on Susan Hightower's phone, and I'm sure I'll hear from her as soon as she lands in Missoula."

"You'll call me?" Annie asked. "If you hear anything at all?"

"Absolutely. And we have officers patrolling the locations we discussed."

Jack gave her his card with his numbers on the front and Annie's numbers printed on the back.

The deputy walked them out to the lobby. "Sheriff Buck Holladay will be here at seven a.m. I suggest you call about eight and get an update."

The three of them shook hands, and Jack steered Annie outside to his car. It was time for his assistant, Gavin LaRue, to get more responsibility on the job site. Because for Jack, Job One, now, was to keep danger away from Annie and Savannah.

The irony did not escape him that his best friend would be arriving in Bitter Falls in something like twelve hours to try to talk him into throwing Marcy into a lake with piranhas.

Good luck with that, Travis. You might as well go fishing while you're here. No piranhas in the

Bitter River.

"Where are we going?" Annie asked as he pulled out of the dirt lot behind the Silver County Courthouse.

"I know you want to be with Savannah," he said, "but I don't want to scare the heck out of Vera by waking her up at two a.m. I'll stay with you at your place for what's left of the night. Deputy Pacheco is right. We have to get some sleep so we're sharp tomorrow."

She said nothing. He glanced over and saw tears spill out of her eyes.

"Annie, it's going to be all right. You and Savannah are not alone."

"I know," she said softly. "That's why I'm crying. Not because I'm scared, but because I'm grateful."

****

Annie lay on her left side on her double bed, wrapped like a burrito in a thermal weave blanket. Jack lay beside her, one arm draped over her waist. She was glad to hear his rhythmic breathing; at least one of them was getting the sleep they both needed so badly.

When they'd trudged into her house, the adrenaline from Delia's calls and the sheriff's department was wearing off and she was sinking into a zombie-like state.

Jack got her to lie down on her bed, still in her jeans and sweatshirt, but she couldn't stop shaking.

"I'm so cold," she'd said, pulling her knees up in almost a fetal position. Jack had wrapped the blanket around her and cuddled against her back.

Now that she was awake, anxiety bloomed, racing madly to every corner of her mind and sapping her ability to reason. Slowly, so as not to wake Jack, she slipped one hand over to her bedside table. From the open prescription bottle, she fished one of the tiny tablets out and placed it under her tongue.

He moved slightly and groaned a little in his sleep, making her smile. He was too tall for the bed, and it was too small in both directions for the two of them. At least, too small for quality sleep. It would be fine for sex. Compared to the couch where they'd made love for the first time, this was an acre.

Face it, anywhere would be fine for sex with Jack. She wished she was the kind of woman who could settle for that. No strings. If she hadn't been so old-fashioned, she could have had a fling with Peter Dylan and moved on, heart intact. Win some, lose some, like her girlfriends all said. Women don't have to wait around for some halfwit prince to ride in.

She hadn't played hard-to-get with Peter. She hadn't played any game at all. She'd told him the truth, that she wasn't into casual sex. She'd had two serious boyfriends, one in college and one after college, and neither one was marriage material. She'd ended up being disappointed in them, and even more disappointed in herself, so she'd sort of sworn off men.

Well, not men, exactly. What she'd sworn off was casual sex, and in today's dating scene, where waiting for sex until the second date was considered a tease, that was tantamount to swearing off men.

Once she'd made her position clear, she expected Peter to disappear. But he was endearingly persistent. They met for lunch, dinner, and concerts when their schedules allowed. He admitted he had no eye for art and counted on her to make small talk for them when he couldn't avoid a museum or gallery show.

At a charity art auction, he gave her the paddle and actually went to sleep sitting up. She bought a watercolor triptych of yachts on Lake Washington that would look better in his office than what he had, a generic mountain scene painted by the thousands in a Chinese art factory.

She went with him to Hawaii with clear ground

rules. Snorkeling, yes; getting better acquainted, yes. Then, somehow, in the tropical moonlight, with "Blue Hawaii" playing softly like the song of the Sirens tempting Ulysses, she'd said yes to marriage. Even now, she remembered Hawaii like a fairy tale. And then, like the old punch line, she woke up married.

As dreadful a mistake as it had been, she couldn't regret it. She had Savannah.

But she couldn't go on with this fling with Jack. She had a child to raise, a construction and furnishing project to complete, and a whole business to create from nothing. She didn't have energy left over for wanting Jack. For adjustment, accommodation. All the drama of being a couple.

She'd moved to Montana to find herself, not to lose herself again.

Wanting Jack Cabrini was a full time job by itself.

She shouldn't have jumped his bones tonight. *What must he think of me? Never mind. I know what he thinks of me.*

The only thing I should focus on, she thought with fierce determination, is keeping Savannah safe.

The pill took effect, and the crazy woman in her head became calm, rational. Instead of running up and down the smoky halls of a hotel yelling, "Nine-one-one, nine-one-one!" she could press three numbers on her phone, walk out the clearly marked exit, and let the professionals do what they're trained to do.

If you can keep your head when all about you are losing theirs and blaming it on you...

Jack's breathing changed, and she could tell he was awake.

"Good morning," she murmured. "I'm ready to unwrap this and see if I've turned into a butterfly."

He kissed her cheek and rolled the other way, off the bed. She rolled over and tossed the blanket away from her.

"Do you want to shower first?" he asked. "I can make the coffee."

"I'll shower in Tess's bathroom. I have to wake her up and tell her all that's happened."

Half an hour later, the three of them sat in the kitchen with mugs of steaming coffee.

Annie called the sheriff's non-emergency number printed on Deputy Pacheco's card. She expected a dispatcher or a deputy to answer, but Buck Holladay picked up himself. As soon as she identified herself, his voice changed from brusque to kindly.

"Ms. Riker, I sent Deputy Pacheco over to your house, on Maple, to fill you in before she goes off duty. She's got two U.S. Marshals with her."

A knock on the front door; Jack answered it.

"They're here, Sheriff," Annie said. "Thank you."

"You feel free to call me back if you have any questions. And I'll be on the horn to you if I get any change of status. This here is a can of worms, that's what it is."

"Good morning, ma'am."

"Good morning, Deputy Pacheco. Thanks for coming over. This is my sister, Tess Riker."

Pacheco introduced Susan Hightower and Mike Hale. Everyone shook, and Tess poured three more mugs of coffee. Jack got one chair from the garage so they could all sit at the dinette table.

Deputy Pacheco's uniform was still as crisp as it had been at midnight, but Annie could see tiny signs of fatigue on her face as she nodded to Hightower and Hale and opened her notebook.

"It looks like we have good news to report," she said.

"Thank God," Annie said.

Jack covered her hand with his and gave it a squeeze.

"We've been out of the loop while traveling,"

Susan Hightower said. "We got to the sheriff's department in time to hear this ourselves."

"Sheldon Roth crossed the border to Canada by car a few minutes before two o'clock this morning. Fingerprints showed he was the driver who left the Chenoweth's Hummer on the Bremerton ferry. The police started looking for alternate means of transportation but didn't have any luck."

"And yet he drove across the border?" Jack asked.

"He has a valid passport and a valid bill of sale for a 2005 Toyota pickup. He crossed as Peter Van Hogen and didn't set off any alarms. He made a reservation on a flight to Paris that leaves," she looked at her watch, "in about two hours."

"The Mounties are waiting for him," Mike Hale said. "Not to arrest him, but to take him into protective custody as a material witness to a homicide."

"What a relief," Annie said. "He wasn't heading this way at all. I guess I overreacted."

Jack saw a look pass between the Deputy U.S. Marshals. Susan Hightower gave an almost imperceptible nod.

"Speaking of homicide," Pacheco continued, "the Bellevue P.D. faxed me a photo of the shooter at the Chenoweth home. The attorney and his wife had a 'nanny cam' to watch a cleaning lady with sticky fingers. The FBI insists they could get the photo clearer, but it's pretty good as is."

She opened a manila folder and placed a grainy black and white photo, eight by ten inches, on the table. Jack watched Annie's face as she studied it. For a long moment, she worried her lip with her teeth, then shrugged.

"I don't have any idea who that is. Peter Dylan and I went to social events together, but he wanted to keep our marriage a secret until he told his troubled son."

She looked up at Susan Hightower. "You worked on the case. You know he didn't have a son. It was just one of his many lies. That lie turned out to be a good thing for me. When he was arrested, the press didn't know about me."

"Well," Susan said, "I certainly guessed wrong. This time the ninety-five percent opinion was correct. He was heading out of the country."

"I'm curious," Annie said. "Why did you think he would come here?"

Again Jack saw the dark look pass between Hightower and Hale.

"We might as well tell you the odd fact that doesn't fit in the package," Susan said. "We looked at his contacts while he was in prison. He made collect calls to a photographer and videographer in Seattle. I checked the records I can access from the original case. Sheldon had a corporate account with Josef Abbas. A detective questioned him, but it was a dead end. Anyway, Mike and I went to see him yesterday. And what we found out you aren't going to like."

Annie looked at Jack, then at Susan. "What?"

"Sheldon was paying Abbas to take photos of your daughter and send them to him via a computer at the prison."

"What?" Annie said, incredulous. "How did this person I never heard of get close enough to take pictures of Savannah? What kind of pictures?"

"Abbas swears it was harmless," Mike said. "Ice cream shop, Quizno's, coming out of church."

"To a computer inside a prison?" Jack asked. "What am I missing here?"

"We're still trying to tie the pieces together," Susan said, "but it looks like he could receive email when he was on a restricted site answering tourists' questions."

"Does Delia Phinney know?" Annie asked.

"Yes. Since last night. She suggested we tell you since we interviewed Abbas."

Annie nodded. "I would never have guessed Sheldon had any interest in Savannah. It makes my skin crawl."

"Did he ever write to you, ask you for a picture of her?" Susan again.

Annie nodded her head slowly. "Twice. I wouldn't answer. Actually, it could have been more than twice. I refused to accept other mail."

"In any event," Susan said, "now you see why I insisted we get on a plane to Montana." She tapped her forehead. "Intuition. Previously a reliable guide."

"I appreciate that you'd go the extra mile," Annie said. "So to speak. Delia Phinney thinks very highly of you both."

"If we're okay here," Deputy Pacheco said, "I'm off duty and ready to sleep."

They stood and shook hands all around again.

"Now that we're in the wilderness," Mike said, "we're taking a couple days off. I'm going fishing."

"I probably ought to use the time to update my resumé," Susan said with a dry laugh. "I didn't just step on toes over this. I ran a steamroller over several feet."

"Would you like to see Albion House?" Tess asked. "Or go horseback riding? You could do both."

"Thanks, Tess," Susan said. "I want to find a motel and get cleaned up. Maybe I'll buy some jeans. Could I take your cell number and call you this afternoon?"

"Sure."

Jack, Annie and Tess watched the three law enforcement officers shake hands again on the sidewalk and get in their cars.

"I'm so relieved," Tess said.

"Me, too," Annie said. "But I'll be more relieved when Sheldon is in custody. There's still a killer looking for him."

"I hope the killer..." Jack's voice slowed and stopped.

"What?" Annie asked. "You hope the killer what?"

"Probably nothing. But the fact that the killer found him at Chenoweth's house implies a leak. I hope it's not someone on the inside."

When he saw the distress on Annie's face, he was sorry he'd said it.

"Everything will be fine," he said. "Let's go get our girls and start this day over again."

In answer, Annie put her arms around his neck and kissed him. "How's that for a way to start the day?"

"Whoa," Tess said, "three's a crowd. I'll be at Albion House. See you two later."

Chapter Fourteen

On the short drive from Vera's home to Albion House, Annie listened to Savannah and Marcy chatter, glad to be back in her normal life. Two hours ago, no, less than that, she'd been ready to grab Savannah and get on a small plane out of Bitter Falls.

Where they'd go she hadn't decided. She simply wanted to be far away, where Sheldon Roth and/or the killer pursuing him couldn't find them.

A new lease on life. Thank you, Lord. Back to cookies and puppies and leaping fearlessly off the diving board. Jack was back to work. She knew he was relieved at the news of Sheldon's impending capture in Canada, but something was still eating at him, something they hadn't had time to discuss. Maybe they could talk when she got to Albion House with the girls.

Meanwhile, cookie recipes were the hot topic of the day. Vera had let the girls bake cookies and had put the idea in their heads to enter the county fair's junior division.

"Aunt Vera said they can't be ordinary cookies," Marcy explained to Annie. "We have to make them stand out. Secret ingredients. Like lavender. We'll have to bake lots of batches, and Vera said the men working at Albion House will be glad to dispose of our failures."

The next topic was dog collars. Rhinestones, or no rhinestones? Annie voted as she knew Jack would, against rhinestones, saying other dogs would make fun of Lady and Katy.

When she'd picked up the girls, Vera had waved

off her thanks, saying the girls had been no trouble.

"None at all," she'd repeated. "Annie, it means so much to me to see Marcy turn around this way. Jack and I can tell her seven ways to Sunday that she's wonderful, but it doesn't cancel the way she's been abused by those people in Denver. It would hurt anyone to be falsely accused and publicly humiliated. But a teenage girl? What kind of monsters are those people? Savannah's hero worship is building Marcy up right when she needs it most."

Now that the cement truck was gone, Annie felt her car was safe in the row of pickups behind the new garage. The girls bounded out and headed for the solarium to sort tiles.

Jack came out of the shell of the garage in time to see them. He smiled and walked to Annie's car, opened her door.

"I wish my paid crew was that eager to get to work," he said.

"I thought you were paying the girls."

"Payment in kind. Time on horseback. Or ponyback, in Savannah's case. I'm running a tab with Tree Autrey."

She picked up a paper sack, rolled tight at the top. "The girls baked these for you."

"Yum. I'm going to—" He was interrupted by his cell phone.

Annie saw irritation—or was that alarm?—flash across his face as he excused himself. As he stepped away, she heard him say, "Travis. What's up?"

She opened the back of her Ford Escape and got her hardhat, leather portfolio, and the unopened mail she'd tossed in at her house. Checking to be sure she had her metal measuring tape and clipboard with a diagram of the solarium, she headed toward the house. As she walked, she opened the top letter.

"Annie?"

She turned back. "Yes?"

The muscles in his jaw were tight; whatever Travis had said wasn't good news to Jack.

"I've got a...situation. Travis is here—"

"In Bitter Falls?"

Jack shrugged. "Yeah. He has some cockamamie idea that he can talk me into letting Marcy get involved with the rapidly deteriorating legal mess in Denver. The three of us have to have a serious talk. He's at my house."

"I see. So you and Marcy—"

"We need to get over there. The immediate problem is that I want to talk to him alone. Before Marcy gets involved."

A little beep of a horn made them turn to see Tess pull in beside Annie's car.

"How about I bring Marcy over in a while? How long do you want?"

He seemed lost in thought. "Thirty minutes?"

"You've got it." She walked over to Tess's car.

"Hey," Tess said. "Where's the munchkin?"

"In the solarium. I'm going to measure the piano platform in there and then take Marcy on an errand. Would you take care of Savannah for a little while?"

"Sure. I'm here to talk to Gavin about the built-in shelves we want behind the front desk. I'll take Savannah to the grocery store with me."

"Thanks."

Half an hour later, Annie drove down the driveway with Marcy in the passenger seat. They turned left on Prescott Street.

"You're taking me to see Travis McGarry, aren't you?"

She looked over at Marcy, sure her surprise was written all over her face. There was an edge to Marcy's voice Annie hadn't heard before. It sounded a little like a challenge.

"Yes, but I didn't know anything about him coming to Montana until half an hour ago. Jack and I talked yesterday evening, at Mr. Randolph's farm, about your trouble in Denver. He said things were beginning to heat up with the district attorney, but I had no reason to think anything was coming up so soon. His request, to drive you to your new house, came as a complete surprise to me."

Marcy seemed to withdraw, and Annie got the message. Marcy didn't believe her. She knew all too well how *that* felt. How many times had she told people she knew nothing about Peter Dylan's other life?

She pulled the car to a sudden stop in the shade of a tree and turned off the engine. Jack wanted Marcy at his house in a few minutes, but he could wait.

She thought of one way to start, discarded that; thought of another way. When she opened her mouth, all she had time to say was, "Marcy, if I—" before the girl snapped at her.

"You just want to be Jack's girlfriend."

"Are you saying I can't be trusted to tell you the truth? That I'm doing and saying whatever Jack wants?"

"Yes, and believe me, you aren't the first." Her lips were in a tight line, but her chin was quivering as she tried to hold back tears.

"Marcy, as people go through life, things happen to them. And those things change them."

She turned in her seat. Marcy stared straight ahead, but Annie knew she was listening.

"If someone acts vicious and hateful to you, you automatically put up a shield. I think that's instinctual. But if someone pretends to be sweet, and you find out she was only using you to get what she wanted, you *learn* not to trust people. I know how that feels."

Marcy shrugged as if to say, *Go on.*

"I've been through some trouble. It's a long story, and I promise I'll explain it to you and answer every question you have. For now we'll have to go with the short version. Six years ago I fell in love with a man in Seattle. We got married, I got pregnant, which was the biggest thrill of my life, and then he got arrested."

"Arrested? Had he done something wrong?"

"His arrest was nothing like what happened to you. He was guilty of a number of crimes. Sheldon had swindled a lot of people out of millions of dollars. And he was married to three women at the same time. Which, as you can instantly figure out, meant I was never legally married."

"Did he go to prison?"

"Yes. He was supposed to go to prison for thirty years, but the judge pulled a switcheroo when he signed the sentencing documents, and it was changed to three ten-year sentences running concurrently. In other words, ten years total. That was five and a half years ago. But four days ago he got out, a fact I discovered three days ago."

"How? Where is he going?"

"Those are two questions I can't answer. But wait, it gets much worse. Last night, in Seattle, he was at the home of his attorney. A man broke in and shot and killed his attorney. From what I've heard, there's no question that the man was trying to kill Sheldon, but he got away. He's on the run now, with the shooter chasing him, and all kinds of police chasing after both of them."

Marcy's jaw dropped, and her eyes widened. "You don't think he'll—I mean, he won't come here, will he?"

"My mind jumped that way as fast as yours did. It's been a long, scary night."

"What about now?"

"This morning at the crack of dawn, a deputy sheriff and two officers from the United States Marshals Service showed up at my house. They said Sheldon Roth got to Vancouver, Canada, under some other name. He made a reservation to fly to Paris."

She looked at her watch. "Right about now the police in Canada are picking him up."

"Why? You said he's out of prison."

"He's what's called a material witness. He saw the shooter kill his attorney. So even if the shooter wasn't out to kill him before, he'll want to kill him now. It's very ugly."

She thought about what Jack had said, that there seemed to be a leak inside law enforcement or Sheldon's attorney's office. The photo of the killer, taken by the nanny-cam, came to her mind. She was sure she didn't know who it was, and yet...a feeling nagged at her that she had, in fact, seen him before.

Marcy seemed to consider what Annie said. "All right, let's go see Travis."

Annie turned on the ignition and headed down Main Street and out the county road toward Jack's place.

"I pretty much know in advance that the two of them will argue about what's best for me," Marcy said, "and neither one of them will listen to me. Jack doesn't want me to testify to anybody about anything. He'd like to put me in a bubble suit and pipe in air to me."

"Do you think Travis feels differently about it? You said they would probably argue."

"Travis and I talked on the phone yesterday." She paused. "He said it might come down to my testimony being the only way Crystal and her mom, and Heather, stop sliming people."

"How did that make you feel?"

"Like I should do it."

"Would you like me to stay for this clash of the titans? Instead of dropping you off? You and I together might get Jack and Travis to shut up and listen to you."

"Dream on." Marcy took in a deep breath and let it out slowly. "If you're willing to try, I guess I've got nothing to lose."

"That's the spirit." She smiled but kept her eyes on the road. "And, by the way, yes, I want to be Jack's girlfriend. I haven't been anybody's girlfriend for a lot of years."

****

Jack gripped the edge of the granite counter in his kitchen and watched his fingers turn white.

"Go ahead," Travis shouted. "Fire me!"

"Don't push me, Travis." He looked out the window over the sink. *Where the hell are they?*

The sooner Travis explained the Denver mess to Marcy, and the sooner he and Marcy made it clear to Travis that he was hired to keep her out of it, the sooner he'd be out of town.

Which was one hell of a sad commentary on his life, wasn't it? His thirty-year friendship with Travis McGarry was teetering on the edge of a toilet bowl. He'd always heard it was a mistake to mix business with friendship—or love—and this proved that old adage true.

"Here she comes."

"Am I going to meet the woman you're so crazy about?"

"How? How do you know anything about Annie? I haven't said a word to you." That was a fact. The only times he'd talked to Travis since meeting Annie Riker—four impossibly short days ago—were to bark at him about the case in Denver. Annie was...well, Annie was a private matter. He couldn't define in his own mind what was happening between them, and he sure as hell wasn't going to discuss it with Travis, the serial lover. His flippant assessment of what Jack was feeling for Annie was the last thing he needed.

"How?" Jack asked again, with as much menace as he could squeeze into three letters.

"Marcy called me yesterday," Travis said.

"What the hell?" He slapped his open hand hard on the counter and made a satisfying, explosive

178

sound. "Marcy doesn't—she doesn't know anything about—" Jack's sputtering rant was cut short by the front door opening.

"Travis, I've missed you so much!" Marcy flew into the room and threw her arms around Travis's neck. He lifted her off the floor and swung her around.

"I'm Annie Riker."

Jack's head swiveled around. He'd thought she would drop Marcy off; that was clearly what he'd communicated. This was no time for a social visit. Nor was it, he thought with genuine regret and a flash of hot memory, the time for romance. Didn't she know he'd think of the two of them on the couch?

Talk about an elephant in the room. Theirs was dark red leather.

He watched Travis shake hands with Annie and ask nicey-nice questions about how the project was coming along and how he hoped Jack was adjusting to his new, downsized career.

"You've got to come see my puppy, Travis—"

"Travis will only be here for an hour, Marcy. He has important business in Denver."

"Actually, I'm planning to stay for the weekend. And don't worry, I'm off the clock. All the advice I give you this afternoon is free."

"And worth every penny," Jack snarled.

"Jack!" Marcy said. To Travis she said, in a conspiratorial voice, "Sounds like somebody needs a time out."

"Thank you for bringing Marcy over, Annie. I'm sure you're in a hurry to get back to Savannah."

"She's with Tess. Marcy invited me to stay for the fireworks here."

"Did she?" He glared at Marcy. "And Travis tells me you called him yesterday. What are you up to?"

"I thought you'd never ask. Let's all take a seat. Travis, can I get you a beer or a soda? Annie?"

They both asked for ice water and moved, along

with Marcy, to the central living room. Jack had no choice but to join them.

Annie looked at the couch and back at him with a provocative smile on her face. A smile he wanted to kiss right off her mouth. She took a seat in the tulip-shaped leather armchair; Travis sat on one end of the couch.

As much as Jack wanted to avoid the scene of the best couple hours of his life, he, too, sat on the couch.

Marcy brought water to the guests and moved the coffee table over so Travis and Annie could reach it more easily. Then she settled on an ottoman facing all three of them. Jack wondered what she'd do next. Offer to put music on the stereo?

"What's the latest on the case?" Marcy asked. "As Vera always says, we're on tenterhooks."

If Travis asks how Vera is, I'll deck him.

He'd already decided to ground Marcy until she went to college.

"The principal of your former school and two members of the board of directors are being deposed today and tomorrow," Travis said. "They're all claiming they had no knowledge of misuse of the school computers by Crystal DeBeers and Heather Janson. Valdez Domingo, the father of Geraldo Domingo, is demanding an FBI investigation of this as a hate crime, and he has a lot of powerful friends."

Annie sipped her water and smiled encouragement to Marcy. She watched Jack rub his forehead as if he had a headache.

She set her glass on the table and reached out to squeeze Marcy's hand. She couldn't tell if the shaking was her hand or Marcy's—or both. To Travis she said, "A hate crime?"

He nodded. "The girls and Luella DeBeers started a wave of extremely nasty allegations that Geraldo, age fifteen and a gifted dancer who has studied classical dance in Spain, is gay. Whether he is or not is none of my business—nor is it anyone else's business. But the attack devastated him. He attempted suicide. The only thing that saved him was that the housekeeper found him in time to get paramedics to the house."

Annie's face went white. "Oh, no. Do you think the FBI will help?"

"I don't know, but the Colorado State Police have opened an investigation, and the district attorney has issued a subpoena for the computers and all related records. Including all complaints filed with the principal about harassment by Crystal and Heather, and Marcy's complaints about organized cheating."

"That's more than I expected," Jack conceded.

"Meanwhile, I have provided copies of all the computer harassment of Marcy by Luella DeBeers pretending to be a student. It was all traceable. And I contacted Domingo Valdez's attorney to make sure he knows."

"Tell him the best part," Marcy urged.

Jack glared at her.

"As you know, when the police dropped the shoplifting charge against Marcy, I kept a certified copy of the store's surveillance tape and sworn statements from the two employees. One of those employees contacted me a few days ago. She said Crystal and Heather have been caught shoplifting at four stores in that mall in the past year. Mall security has the proof."

"See?" Marcy said to Jack. "It won't be my word against everyone else."

"That's not to say it's a slam dunk," Travis continued. "The attorneys for the mall will do everything short of sacrificing their firstborn to keep the mall out of this. So they're sitting on it for now."

"If it goes to trial?" Jack asked. "What then?"

Travis chuckled. "That's why God made little

green apples. And subpoenas."

"I want to be deposed," Marcy said. "And I'm willing to go back to Denver to do it."

"Being deposed in a nice little room with soft furniture is one thing, Marcy," Jack snapped. "But if this goes to a trial, you'll be tabloid fodder. Those vermin will chew you to pieces."

"If nobody stands up to them," Marcy said, "people like Cruella DeBeers and Crystal and Heather will get away with everything, just like they always have."

She stood, her hands in fists at her side and her face red with the effort of not crying.

"No!" Jack shouted. "I don't want you dragged into it."

"Jack!" Annie stood up and put her arms around Marcy. "Marcy is being brave, and she deserves your support."

"She doesn't deserve to be maligned and harassed. And that's what will happen. I love her too much to let it happen. And I'm her parent. Not Travis, and not you!"

The air was thick with tension.

"Travis," Annie said, "could I change seats with you, please?"

"Sure."

Annie sat on the couch and pulled Marcy close beside her. Fixing her gaze on Jack, she said, "I want to tell you something that happened to me."

She squeezed Marcy's shoulders and smiled at her.

"When the man I knew as Peter Dylan was arrested, I was in a state of shock. His financial crimes were horrible. Many people lost their life savings. Four pension funds lost millions, and at least six charities closed their doors, completely wiped out. Of course that was all painful to me. To think I'd been with him, loved him, conceived a baby with him. And he was a stranger. No, much worse than that. He was a monster."

She sighed and collected her thoughts. "The day after he was arrested, I found out he was married to two other women besides me. He was charged with bigamy along with other crimes. I had to endure painful questioning, over and over. Believe me, Marcy, I know what it's like to tell the truth and be called a liar."

She took a sip of water. "Finally, the prosecutors believed I knew nothing about his financial house of cards or his other wives. They wanted me on the stand to get a conviction on the bigamy charge. They said that would show the jury what they were dealing with before the prosecution got into the incredibly difficult world of his financial swindles."

Travis nodded. Annie figured he could probably see what was coming.

"But I refused to testify," she said. "Refused! I said he was a bigamist when he married the second woman, so let her testify. I wanted to get out of the circus. Nothing they said would change my mind, and they didn't want to call me as a hostile witness and have the jury angry at the prosecutor."

She took a deep breath and exhaled. "Since I was not testifying at his trial, I attended the day his two wives were on the stand."

Marcy pressed her hand on Annie's, telling her silently to go on.

"The second wife was extremely nervous on the witness stand. The judge had to stop the questioning four or five times for her to regain her composure. Every time, the defense lawyer came at her harder. He was merciless, calling her a liar and a pathetic woman who just wanted attention. He found holes in her memory of dates and events and kept coming back to them, trying to trip her up. He completely destroyed her on the stand. When she stepped down, almost collapsing from the strain, the lawyer got the charge of bigamy dropped."

She looked into Marcy's eyes.

"I sat there, knowing I could have changed the trial. I could have saved that woman from the public gutting she endured. But I thought only of myself and my reputation. I was no better than people who witness a child shot in the street and won't identify the shooter."

"Marcy is thirteen," Jack said solemnly.

"And wiser than I was at twenty-three. Braver, too."

Marcy sniffed and wiped fat tears off her cheeks. Annie handed her the napkin from beside her water glass.

"I promised myself I wouldn't cry," Marcy said, looking from Travis to Annie, but avoiding Jack's cold-steel gaze. "That's the fastest way," she sniffed, then sniffed again, "to get Jack to clam up and turn his back. But now here I go, crying like a big baby."

Annie folded Marcy tight against her and held her shoulders as she shook and let out a lot of pain.

Jack rose and went to the kitchen. He came back with a beer and a box of tissues. Saying nothing, he handed the box to Annie. She pulled out a fistful of tissues and gave them to Marcy.

She watched Jack stand at the front picture window, staring out but probably not focused on anything. He tipped up the can and drank about half the beer in one swallow. He turned and met her eyes.

Smile. If eyes could speak, hers must surely be shouting. *Please smile at me, Jack. Please accept the love I'm offering.*

He turned his back, and she knew exactly how Marcy felt.

I should leave. God knows I have enough problems of my own.

But she couldn't move. She couldn't leave while Marcy needed to lean on her.

That was the real issue here, wasn't it? Marcy

the girl and Marcy the woman-to-be needed someone to lean on. She needed unconditional love. Jack loved his little sister very much, but he thought by strong-arming external threats, by keeping her out of harm's way, he was doing all he needed to do.

The *Sleeping Beauty* school of parenting.

Marcy took a deep breath, tried to laugh, and pulled away.

"I got your blouse wet." She pressed the wad of tissues to her face one more time and slid a couple feet away on the couch.

Impulsively, Annie stood and took Marcy by the hand. Tugging her to her feet, she led her across the room toward her brother.

Jack turned, blinking his eyes. His wet eyes.

Must be bright sunshine, Annie thought. The old reliable guy reason.

Annie gave Marcy a gentle shove, and Jack opened his arms.

Her face against his broad, solid chest, Marcy's voice was muffled, but Annie heard what she said.

"I want you to be proud of me."

"I am, sweetheart. I am. I'm just lousy at showing it."

"Jack?" Marcy looked up at him. "That's not all. I want to be proud of myself."

He squeezed her tight against him, and the two of them rocked back and forth.

"Travis," he said at last, "let's get started. Call the D.A. and see when he wants us in Denver. We have a lot of prep to do before we pour the concrete around those lying bitches."

Annie walked straight to the front door, out to her car, and drove away. She needed to have a certain little girl in her arms. She needed to squeeze her into jelly.

Things would be hard for Marcy and Jack; the legal battle and inevitable public exposure that loomed would exhaust them. Jack wasn't making any of that up, nor was he exaggerating it.

And every time it gets really bad, he'll probably think of me and how I interfered in his life.

How's that for a fairy tale? Not so good.

Because I made him look weak.

At least, that was how a tough guy like Jack would see it. The last thing he'd ever believe was that the strongest man, the kind of man that women truly love, is the man who doesn't run from emotion. Women admire a man's broad shoulders, narrow waist, watermelon biceps, and buns of steel, but what they want is to be held gently. To be listened to. To be treasured for who they are, not for how they improve his social standing or self-image.

Jack Cabrini would undoubtedly be a more sensitive man after this—which, to Annie, was synonymous with a *better* man—but it wouldn't be with her.

She wiped tears from beneath her eyes. "It's okay," she said aloud. "I'll be fine."

She'd outgrown fairy tales a long time ago.

Haven't I? Well? Haven't I?

If not, she'd better outgrow such fluff right now.

Why?

"Because!" she said, in the exact tone she used to halt one of Savannah's nerve-fraying strings of *Why, Mommy? Why?*

Because...

She shivered, unaccountably cold. Unaccountably—lonely.

Because, as life plans go, getting kissed—even by a certified prince—is vastly overrated.

Chapter Fifteen

Susan Hightower swung her right leg over the back of the saddle and removed her left foot from the stirrup. She landed nimbly on both feet and winced at a sharp pain when her denim jeans rubbed her inner thighs.

"My plan to emigrate and join the Royal Canadian Mounted Police requires more thought," she said to Tess Riker. "And salve. Lots of salve."

Mike Hale had the nerve to laugh. He could afford to laugh, since he'd refused to get on board a horse. To...mount a horse. Whatever.

Susan patted Majesty on his neck and, with mincing steps, climbed the wooden steps to the vast porch of the Rocking Star Guest Ranch. She curled her lip and growled like a lioness as she snatched the long-necked bottle of beer out of Mike's hand and tipped it up.

"Hey, that's mine."

She handed him back the empty bottle. "You're right. It is."

Gingerly, she sat in a wicker chair and looked out over the spectacular view of the Montana wilderness. Tess Riker walked toward the barn and handed Majesty's reins to a cowboy. Or, Susan corrected herself, to a horseboy. Horseman.

"What's going on?" She didn't bother to explain her question. Mike understood exactly what she wanted to know.

She'd tried her cell phone seven or eight times on the trail ride and gotten "No Signal Available" every time. Now the battery was dead and she'd have to plug it into the car charger.

Crap. The car was about half a mile away. Divide by two. Two thousand six hundred feet. Divide by two. One thousand three hundred steps. With the starched denim of her new jeans rubbing her inner thighs like steel wool on raw meat.

"Mike?" she snapped. "What the hell is going on?"

"Brick wall. Nobody will tell me anything."

She swore. "Give me your phone."

He complied and said he was going inside to get another beer.

"Good idea. Get one for yourself, too."

She tried five numbers in Seattle and got five "Leave a Message" recordings. She stared at the floor of the porch, a little concerned that her eyes might cause combustion of the dry wood.

Mike returned with two bottles, and she traded his phone for a bottle. She took a long swig of the cold beer and burped like a ten-year-old boy. "I will never drink a martini again. Beer is the elixir of the gods."

"No luck on the phone, I presume? I called the local sheriff. He couldn't get any information either."

"I have an excellent idea for how to get information, but the number I need is on a business card in my purse. In the car. Seven miles away."

He shrugged. "All right. I'll go get your purse."

"I have a better idea. Go move the car to the handicapped parking space right there. That's as far as I can walk. And I've got to charge my phone."

"I'll do it for ten dollars."

"Deal."

"And ninety dollars not to put a video on YouTube of you walking like you've got a cactus up your ass." He held up his phone and waggled it back and forth.

"All right, one hundred dollars, but I get to fire my weapon at your feet if you don't go fast enough."

"I hope your next partner is a real bitch."

"Ah, Mikey, don't you want to work with me? You can flip the burgers and I'll sweetly ask, 'Sir, do you want fries with that?'"

Ten minutes later, sitting in the passenger seat of their rental car, she reached Edie Chenoweth, attorney and daughter of the dead Isaac Chenoweth.

Two minutes later, she knew what no one wanted to admit. Sheldon Roth, the man with a shiny new passport and reservations to Paris, hadn't shown up at the Vancouver Airport. There had been no sign of him anywhere since he drove into Canada at approximately midnight. No sign, no news. That is, nothing until a short time ago.

At four-thirty p.m., mountain daylight time, a Toyota pick-up driven by a U.S. citizen named Peter van Hogen had crossed the Canadian border into the U.S. at an almost totally deserted crossing on the extreme southeastern edge of British Columbia.

He'd been in Montana for the better part of an hour.

****

Jack arrived at the house on Maple Street at seven-thirty. Since six o'clock, he'd been on the phone every fifteen minutes with either Tess or the U.S. Marshals.

At six Tess had called him. Had he heard anything from Annie?

"No. Why? What's up?"

Her answer had whipped him down and up like a bungee jump off a high bridge. Sheldon Roth was probably in Montana, she said. And Annie wasn't answering her phone.

Annie had picked up Savannah at their house on Maple at eleven-thirty, Tess said. She'd packed a bag the size of a carry-on with swimsuits, pajamas, and one change of clothes each. She'd said that the two of them needed to get away from stress and strain for a few hours. They might be home at bedtime, or they might stay overnight on the road.

"She came back inside and got beach towels," Tess had added. "I think she was going to a hot spring. She didn't say the name of it, or where it is, just that she saw it in a magazine several months ago. I know there are at least a dozen hot springs in this part of Montana and Idaho. Lots more if you go as far as Wyoming."

"Hot springs," he said, scouring his memory for any he'd heard of. Aside from Mammoth Hot Springs in Yellowstone, he couldn't think of any.

"I thought," Tess said, "she'd call you."

"No," he'd repeated woodenly. "I haven't heard from her. I've called, but I didn't get an answer."

"I'll let you know as soon as she calls."

"Thanks, Tess. I appreciate that."

He'd called Annie's cell four times in the second hour after she left his house. The first hour he was too gob-smacked by what Travis and Marcy had set out before him as necessary preparation for the big fight to come.

And—*be honest, for a change*—he was too proud to call her. He'd always choked on humble pie.

When he'd heard the immediate voicemail message, "Annie Riker is not available," he'd left a terse, "This is Jack. Please call me." The second, third and fourth times the message came on immediately, meaning her phone was not turned on, he'd said nothing, but each time his heart sank lower.

His words that morning—and what was worse, the tone of his voice—ate at him like acid. He'd been so involved in saving face, in being tough Jack Cabrini, the man with the answers, that he'd forgotten to listen to his heart.

The afternoon at Albion House had been crazy busy, with three electricians making megabucks for an hour of cleaning their fingernails, while they waited for the plumbers to get their part done. Inefficiency drove Jack insane.

Annie Riker drove him insane, too.

Insane with wanting.

With regret at his sharp, cold words.

And now insane with worry. *Where the hell is she? And why won't she answer her phone?*

Truth was, he was chagrined but not surprised that Annie wouldn't take his calls. But why not answer her sister? She must be in such a dead zone for cell phones that it was a waste of battery to even have it on. Nowadays people think everyone they know is one press of the Talk button away, but cell phones can let you down. He'd discovered that a few weeks ago when the phone charger in his truck's cigarette lighter failed. He'd checked his voicemail, heard that he had six messages. But before he could listen to the second one, the words "Low Battery" flashed on the screen, and it went black. Dead.

He stepped onto the porch, gave one knock on the screen door, and walked inside.

"Good evening, sir." Deputy Pauline Pacheco was back on duty. She stood as he entered the small living room.

Jack shook her hand, and Mike Hale's, and Susan Hightower's. No, they all said. They had no news.

"Well, a modicum of news," Susan said. "The FBI enhanced the nanny-cam photo of the shooter. I faxed this to you at Albion House."

"Sorry," Jack said. "I didn't see it."

Susan held out a semi-glossy sheet of fax paper with a clear black and white image. The man was about sixty, white, unshaven in a Skid Row way. Salt and pepper facial hair. He wore a suit that Goodwill Industries would say *"No, thanks"* to as a donation. His face said Rage. The look in his eyes reminded Jack of the character in the movie *Network* who told everyone in America to go to their windows, lean out, and shout, "I'm mad as hell, and I'm not gonna take this anymore!"

Clearly, this was not a hit man. The rage was personal.

Susan voiced his thoughts. "That's good news and bad news. A professional hit man could follow Roth like a shadow. Like a python in the Everglades. But this guy would set off every motion detector in Washington, Idaho and Montana."

"I disagree," Jack said. "He looks crazy, and people look the other way."

Susan nodded. "There is something to what you say."

Jack scratched his chin. "Can you track Annie's cell phone?"

"Sprint is cooperating, but she hasn't turned it on since one-fifty," Deputy Pacheco said. "It was on for less than five minutes. One call made to voicemail. She was picked up by a tower near St. Regis, on I-90."

Mike Hale spoke up. "There's a good tourist information center there, but it's closed. I'm working on getting in touch with the manager."

Tess handed Jack a cup of coffee. "Maybe it's a good thing that Annie and Savannah are out of town. I mean, if Sheldon is coming here to find her. And from what you've said," she nodded to Susan, "the crazy shooter knows she lives here."

The coffee was strong and bitter, which perfectly suited Jack's mood. He set his laptop on the corner of the dinette table and pulled up a chair. Searching hot springs, he threw out their names to Tess, hoping she'd recall what had been a casual mention. No luck.

He made phone calls to four that were a reasonable distance from St. Regis. Three calls were answered by machines giving generic hours and location; no telling how long it would be until his messages were heard. The fourth was not a working number.

Two more springs were simply spots in the

forest for people willing to hike long distances. Thinking of Savannah, Jack ruled those out.

Deputy Pacheco sat beside him and smoothed out his map of the region. She glanced at his screen and back at the map. "I've heard of this one."

"That's the one with no working number."

"Makes sense. The owners got sued for something and went out of business. The National Forest Service is trying to get new operators in. Someone with enough money to fix it up. Let me try something."

He angled the computer toward her, and her fingers snapped across the keys. She pulled up a site and dialed a number on her cell. He listened to her side of the conversation and wrote down the number she repeated.

Again she dialed. Again she explained who she was and what she was looking for. This time she wrote down the phone number someone gave her. Another call; another run-through of her identification and her request for information about a woman and little girl.

"They were there?" she said, sitting straight as a flagpole. Jack leaned forward, checking the location on his screen. Tess, Susan and Mike formed a huddle by the table. "How long ago?"

Jack watched Pacheco's face.

"Dropped? I don't understand." Her face fell. "Oh, sure. Did she say anything as they left? Anything that would indicate whether she was looking for a place to spend the night?" She listened, then added, "When will Joaquin be back? I need to speak with him as soon as possible. Does he have a cell phone?"

She held up her pen, and Jack slid the pad of paper in front of her.

"You've been a big help, Mrs. Cruz. I'd appreciate it if you'd write my number down in case you think of anything else."

The deputy glanced around the ring of faces and settled on Tess Riker. "They were there, swimming. Savannah dropped the cell phone in the pool."

A muffled chorus of curses popped out.

"We have the same kind of phone," Tess said. "Not waterproof. She won't have any way to call out."

"What about retrieving messages?" Jack asked.

Tess thought about it. "She can retrieve her messages from another phone by putting in the code. But since her purpose was to get away from stress, I doubt that she would."

"So much for tracking her phone," Jack said, expelling a lungful of air through barely parted lips.

"Don't be too discouraged," Pacheco said. "I have the number of the young man who talked to her at the desk of Renewal Hot Springs. And we can get a BOLO out for her car." She took her notepad from her shirt pocket and recited the license number. "First, I'll talk to Joaquin."

A few minutes later, they knew Annie had talked about going to Big Fork, but that she'd taken a narrow road to the northeast instead, toward a trailhead to a primitive hot spring. The scenic byway was a loop that eventually led back to the interstate highway.

"No," Tess said emphatically. "She wouldn't go to that hot spring. Ever since she heard of a toddler who ran up a trail ahead of his family and got eaten by a cougar, she's been paranoid about the woods. She wouldn't take Savannah on a hike without a Mardi Gras Mummer's Band marching into the woods ahead of them."

She pressed two keys on her cell phone and waited; Jack heard the ringing. "I'm going to tell her we have an emergency here, so if she retrieves her messages from any other phone she'll call me right away."

She listened, then swore under her breath. "Her

mailbox is full. I can't leave another message."

"Our best chance is the Be On Look Out," Pacheco said. "I'll get it started."

Chapter Sixten

Annie would swear the muscles in her shoulders and upper back must be visible as fist-sized knots. Only the business-related urgency of the mail she'd left in the solarium at Albion House was enough to keep her foot on the gas pedal and her hands on the wheel.

She could have called Tess and asked her to meet tomorrow with the bride and her mother. The bride-to-be, from Los Angeles, and her mother, from Dallas, could only be in Bitter Falls for two hours. They had to make their wedding venue decision by close of business tomorrow. Dallas time.

The wedding in mid-October would fill Albion House and the Rocking Star Guest Ranch to the rafters. Not only was the Joslin-Bader wedding excellent business by itself, but the bride was a famous dress designer. She'd fallen in love with western Montana when she was a little girl and always thought she'd get married there. Now that she was making good on her plan, her wedding would draw priceless publicity.

For two reasons, Annie decided to handle the meeting herself. First, she had to stop dumping things on Tess. She could deal with business, Savannah, and Jackson T. Cabrini on her own. In fact, digging into the myriad business decisions would help her get over her infatuation with Jack. And she was utterly, totally, absolutely determined to get over him. The fling was flung. The genie must go back in the bottle.

The glass slipper didn't fit.

The second reason to hurry back to Bitter Falls

"emerged" when Savannah lifted Annie's dripping cell phone from the exquisite mineral-laden water of Renewal Hot Springs.

She turned now on Prescott Street and looked up at the edifice of the hundred-year-old mansion. The railings of the veranda had been removed for the time being, and the first layer of scaffolding abutted the main floor. Where faded black trim used to border the tops of all the windows, now she saw only sad off-white gashes, as if the house had suffered a painful and irrevocable eyebrow wax job.

All the windows on the first and second floors of the main part of the house were papered over. Soon the scaffolding would be higher and the third-floor windows would also be prepped for whiter-than-white spray paint. Once that was completed and the paint dried, the trim, as black and shiny as patent leather shoes, would be reattached. The solarium, with its problematic window replacement running behind schedule, wouldn't be painted until the end of June.

She hoped Jack would be gone this late in the day. She wasn't sorry she'd stood up to him on Marcy's behalf, but at the same time she was sick at her stomach about it. All afternoon she'd been sipping lemon-lime soda, trying to quell the nausea.

The object of her anger and regret wasn't Jack Cabrini. It was herself. Was she truly so needy she'd make love with a man she hardly knew? Was she so gullible? Again?

In other words, had she learned nothing from falling like a stone gargoyle off a cathedral for Peter Dylan?

Savannah had slumped into deep sleep in the backseat after their soak at Renewal Hot Springs. Annie would gladly have napped, too, but she had to drive. They should have named the place Enervation Hot Springs.

Soak here in water guaranteed to sap your

strength, vigor and central nervous system function.

She grinned. *Renewal* had a lot more customer appeal.

Savannah was awake now, singing the alphabet song to herself as she colored in the Disney Princesses coloring book that Vera had given her.

"Mommy, how many days until Lady comes to live with us?"

Annie reached the top of the driveway, at the rear of the mansion, and relief washed over her. Jack's truck wasn't there.

"Twelve days. That means we have a lot of work to do. We have to buy a crate and a book on how to housebreak a puppy."

"And a bed, like the one we saw at the pet store. And doggie toys, and dog food..." Savannah continued the list.

Hmmm. Jack's truck was gone, but so was every other truck and car. Annie was used to seeing workmen outside, wrapping things up, locking tools in their trucks, until the last light faded.

"Let's go inside and get the mail before it gets too dark to see."

"We can turn the lights on."

She pulled the car near the back door and went inside, Savannah at her heels. In the kitchen she reached over her head and turned the knob on the portable light that hung from a hook, the bulb they called the Inquisition Light. *Click.* Nothing.

"I just remembered," she told Savannah. "All the power is off until tomorrow or the day after." She couldn't recall the exact reason Jack had mentioned. Something about a new, deeper plumbing trench and danger of electrocution.

"It's a good thing our customers are visiting in the daytime tomorrow."

"Is the bride really pretty?" Savannah asked as she followed Annie through the dark hallway. "Will she have a flower girl?"

The solarium caught the last light of sunset, and Annie could see the stack of mail on the piano platform. What a dumb place to leave it. If she hadn't opened it on her way into the house earlier in the day, she might have missed the important news about Kendra Joslin and her mom passing through town tomorrow.

"I'm sure she's pretty. I don't know about flower girls."

Flower girls were a hot topic with Savannah since Tess told her she'd wear a long, frilly dress with a satin bow and carry a pink basket. She'd walk in front of Tess at her wedding, scattering rose petals on a white carpet.

"Mommy, can I go get Missy Mermaid? I left her in the lilac garden."

"I'll walk out there with you in a minute. I don't want you falling in a trench. But I just remembered my customer said she'd fax me a list of questions. I hope she sent it before they cut off the power in here."

She picked up the mail and checked the tray of the fax machine they'd set up on the serving bar. There was enough light to make out a typed list with handwritten notes in the margin.

Beneath it was a photograph. It registered in her mind that it was the same photo she'd seen that morning, the photo of the man who shot and killed Isaac Chenoweth. She turned it to catch the faint light. It was measurably more distinct than the first photo. In this one she could see the fury in the man's eyes.

What had been a vague feeling that she'd seen the man before was now cold certainty.

He was the father of Sheldon Roth's second wife, the young woman who went on the witness stand and was ripped apart by Isaac Chenoweth. When Gina Thorne collapsed in tears, her father had to be removed from the courtroom by the bailiff.

It had been one of the worst days of Annie's life—and she wasn't the one on the stand.

Sheldon Roth, a.k.a. Peter Dylan, a.k.a. The Defendant, had turned in his seat and skewered her with his blue-green eyes. Liquid nitrogen was warmer than the eyes of the man she'd loved, married—and by whom she was pregnant.

"Hello, Annie."

Her heart froze. Her breath stopped. She thought of computer graphics that explode an image into a thousand fragments, then revolve and spin, reassembling the image.

"And this must be Savannah." The man's voice again. "You're even prettier than your pictures."

Savannah grabbed her leg and hid her face close to Annie's jeans. Annie pressed her right hand against Savannah's shoulder, the automatic gesture for assurance. The pat-pat that said *It's okay.*

But it wasn't okay. She glanced down and stared into her daughter's blue-green eyes. The pupils were wide in the faint light. Wide, to gather light like a pinhole camera. Wide, to gather information and details. What would happen now? What would be imprinted on her memory of this moment?

"My name is Peter."

Annie's eyes flew to his face. Why Peter instead of Sheldon? Then she recalled that his new, unaccountably valid passport called him Peter van Hogen.

Eight or nine remarks flew through Annie's mind, each trailing *Don't say that in front of Savannah!* like an *Eat at Joe's* banner behind a beach biplane. She settled for the blandest three words she could put together.

"What a surprise."

Please. Her eyes pled what her voice could not say. *Please don't tell her you're her father.*

"You're shy," he said, squatting so he was eye level with Savannah.

What a charmer.

How many times had Annie heard those words about Seattle bachelor Peter Dylan? Not until he was arrested did she think of "charmer" in the context of a snake charmer. One who pipes a hypnotic tune as a King Cobra lifts and waves its regal, lethal head. A cobra with blue-green eyes.

"I heard you were in Canada," Annie said.

He looked up and chuckled. "The climate didn't agree with me." He stood and shook the kinks out of his legs.

"I wouldn't think Montana would be good, either." She heard a car, or truck, shift gears out by the street. Was it coming up the long, sloping driveway around the west end of the mansion? Or simply crossing the low ridge on Prescott Street and heading toward the river? Had Peter heard it?

He turned his back and walked toward the windows that faced the south, and Annie took the opportunity to crane her neck, looking outside. Nothing. The vehicle was out of sight.

"I had a crazy notion I could talk you into, uh, traveling with me." His hands jammed in the pouch of his black warm-up jacket, he strolled back to face her. "You and Savannah. But that was before things got so complicated in Seattle."

"I'm sure you need to go right away, to catch a flight. A lot of people want to talk to you." She held out the photo she'd found in the tray of the fax machine.

He moved with the quickness of a cat to take it from her fingers and angled it toward what was left of the sunset's glow.

"Rotten luck," he said, with no emotion.

Annie thought as she had many times how Peter's cool detachment had drawn her into his web. It had been heady when, in Hawaii, the Ice Man had seemed to melt. She'd thought she was watching a man fall in love for the first time. What woman could resist such a pull? Later, when the glittering-ice-by-moonlight had become a mud puddle in the floodlights of a hundred TV cameras, she knew the truth.

She wasn't the Ice Man's first love. Nor was she his second.

She'd simply been the next in line.

"You're right," he said. "I need to go. I have a long trip ahead of me. And the people who agreed to these terms want to renege."

Annie listened intently but couldn't hear a car door or footsteps. If a car or truck had, in fact, come up the driveway, the driver might be looking at the garage, or the gazebo.

"Savannah and I were about to leave," she said. "Why don't we follow you out the back?"

She sensed a change in the air, as if someone had entered the room. If it was Tess, or Jack, or any of the workmen who'd arrived and seen her car out in back of the dark house, they'd call out to her, but no one said a word.

Instead of relief that someone was coming, she felt...prickly fear.

She glanced over Peter's shoulder and saw no one. The room was dark enough that she couldn't make out anything away from the south-facing windows. To get to her car she'd have to cross the room, go down the long, dark back hallway, through the kitchen and the framed mudroom. It would be faster to get outside through the entryway and front door.

Or—through a window. Two of the large window spaces had no glass. If it were only her, she could throw herself outside that way. But she couldn't do it with her daughter.

Savannah placed her hand in hers, and Annie gave it a gentle squeeze. As she did so, she didn't take her eyes off Peter's face.

"How did you get here, Peter? I didn't see a car."

"I parked my truck behind the garage. This is quite a place you inherited."

Annie saw an opportunity and took it. "Have you seen it from the front? I'll show you."

Clutching tightly to her daughter's hand, she strode toward the entryway by the shortest path, passing between Peter and the hardwood serving bar.

His left arm shot out and blocked her. She stopped and swallowed hard to force down the fear. That's when she heard the sound from the ink-black hallway to the kitchen. The unmistakable sound of a round being chambered in a gun.

Peter turned slowly toward the sound. His right hand came slowly out of the pouch on his jacket. Something was in his hand. Something she couldn't make out in the darkness.

She backed up alongside the serving bar; Savannah moved beside her as if they were attached from her hip down. As much by memory as feel, she knew they were even with the walk-through space that led behind the bar. With both hands on Savannah's shoulders, she guided her into what would be a small galley.

The thick wood that long ago graced the bar of a saloon in Virginia City, Nevada would protect Savannah from bullets. But what would protect her from the kind of terror she'd never be able to forget?

Annie knelt in the opening and whispered, "Sit down. Don't make a sound. Shhhh." Then she stood. Her eyes were used to the darkness, but a black hole is still a black hole.

"This is where it ends," said a man from the far side of the room.

"Not for me," Peter said.

A gunshot less than six feet away nearly deafened Annie, and she threw her body into the galley space, knocking Savannah to the rough subflooring and covering her. A second shot; a third.

Two men yelling. No, more than two. Where did they come from? Running feet.

"Stop!" yelled a woman. "U.S. Marshals."

"Put down your weapon!" A man's voice.

More running. Annie grabbed the top of the bar and lifted herself high enough to see over it. All the sound had moved toward the back of the mansion. Suddenly, the red and blue light of police cars lit up the ceiling. The wail of sirens climbed the hill, and she could tell two or three cars had gone to the rear. Enough flashing light was left from a car stopped in front of Albion House for her to stand and survey the room.

Relief washed over her that she wasn't looking at any dead or bleeding bodies. Whoever had pulled the gun on Peter had either not fired, or had missed.

Sudden scuffling of feet in the entryway sent Annie back to a crouch. Madly, she waved her arms around, searching for a weapon. Nothing. No tools left behind; no loose sections of wood when the workmen had stripped away the old cabinet doors on the wall behind the bar.

Then her fingers closed on what she needed. With both hands, she prepared the top of the weapon as she'd learned to do in safety classes. Balanced on her ankles, she whispered *Shhhh* again to Savannah. The footfalls came closer.

"I'm taking her with me," Peter said, stepping into the walking space between the galley and the solarium's public area.

Roughly, he shoved Annie backward, and she fell awkwardly, striking her head against a crossbar in the cabinetry.

"Mommy!"

With one hand, Annie reached for Savannah. The other hand held fast to the weapon. For a moment Savannah clutched her hand tight. Then, suddenly, she was pulled away, out of the galley.

"Mommy!"

Annie shot to her feet and aimed the fire extinguisher away from her at chest level. Peter took the blast in his face and swore, letting go of Savannah. In the split second she'd gained, Annie screamed for help, grabbed her daughter off the floor as if she weighed five pounds, and ran with superhuman speed toward the gaping window space. Like a torpedo, she dove through the space, holding Savannah tight. They hit the ground and rolled.

As soon as she felt the earth beneath her, Annie was up and running down the hill. She held Savannah in front of her like a log.

"Annie!" Jack materialized at her left and took Savannah out of her arms. "It's all right. It's over."

Her body, which had been an Olympic Gold Medal contender moments ago, collapsed at the knees. As neatly as a pocketknife, she folded to the ground.

"Mommy!" Savannah shrieked, more in horror to see Annie collapse than she'd displayed inside the house. "Mommy!"

"I'm all right, sweetheart. My legs are too shaky to stand up, that's all." She heard the door of the police car at the street slam shut.

"Savannah!" Marcy's voice was close. "Annie! Are you all right?"

Jack knelt and Savannah stood, wrapping her arms around her mom and crying. Jack's strong arms surrounded both of them, then loosened to enclose Marcy, too. So many arms were wrapped every which way, there no way to tell who was hugging whom the hardest. And no way to tell which eyes provided the most tears.

"It's all over," Jack murmured again. "Thank God you're all right."

Chapter Seventeen

Annie opened her eyes and felt her heart clutch suddenly as if squeezed. The room was dark, but light filtered under the door, and she heard the reassuring, calm voice of her sister.

Her right arm was stiff from pressure, but it was welcome pressure—the shoulders of her safe, sleeping daughter. She kissed her forehead and cheeks and slowly reclaimed her arm. Savannah rolled to her right and settled her head against the pillow.

Annie scooted down in the bed and got to her feet. An awful wave of dizziness and nausea made the room spin, and she bumped against her dresser.

The door flew open, and Jack gathered her into his arms. Silently, he backed out of the room and pulled the door almost closed behind them.

"I was afraid of this when they let you leave the hospital," he said.

She opened her eyes, blinking in the light of the kitchen, and found herself sandwiched between Jack and Tess. Standing by the kitchen counter, each with a beer in hand, were the U.S. Marshals. Annie couldn't think of their names.

Gently, Jack placed her in a chair. Tess handed her a glass of ice water.

"What did you say?" Annie muttered. She sipped the water. "What hospital? Why?"

"You have a concussion," Tess said. "You got a big whack on the back of your head. We promised the doctor we'd check you every hour all night if he'd let you come home. How many fingers am I holding up?"

Annie sighed. "Four?"

"Good job. Does your head hurt?"

"Do puppies pee? Of course my head hurts. But confusion hurts more. What happened?" She looked from Tess to Jack and then to the marshals. Their first names came to her. Susan and Mark, or Mack. No, Mike. "What happened to Peter? Is he—?"

She couldn't say the words.

"He's alive." Susan sat across from her. "He took a round in the neck, in and out, but it missed the artery. They stabilized him at the hospital here and took him by ambulance to Missoula."

"And the other man?" Annie put her hand over her mouth, and Tess appeared at her side with a wastebasket. She sat rigidly still until the urge to retch passed.

"It's right here if you need it," Tess said.

Mike-the-Marshal answered her question. "Demetri Thorne suffered a heart attack at the scene. He's in critical condition at your local hospital. If he recovers, he'll be charged with the homicide of Isaac Chenoweth."

"He's the father of—" Annie's voice failed her.

"Of Roth's second wife," Susan said. "Gina Thorne had to be institutionalized for mental breakdown. Her father had just visited her when he found out Roth had been released."

"I don't see how...I mean, how did he follow him to Montana? How could he...?" She waved her hands, unable to frame the questions that battered her mind.

Images from Albion House flashed in her mind like a slide show with no order. Jack taking Savannah from her arms. The sound of the gunshots. Three? Had she heard three? The horror of feeling Savannah pulled from her grip by Peter.

Her daughter's scream of terror.

She buried her face in her hands, wanting the images to stop.

"You need to go back to bed, Annie," Jack said gently.

She felt his arm around her waist. Taking in a lungful of air, she sighed. "Not until you tell me one thing."

"What's that?" Jack whispered as he kissed her cheek and pressed her against him.

"How did any of you know where I was? How did you know I needed help?"

Jack moved a chair and sat beside her, not letting go of her hands. "Susan? You can explain it better than I can."

Annie looked across the table. "How did you know?"

"Mike and I came to Bitter Falls because I had a hunch Sheldon Roth would try to see you. When the FBI said he'd gone to Canada to catch a plane to France, it looked like I was way off the map. Around that point, you left town for a few hours. But—he didn't show up at the Vancouver airport. And the FBI shut off all information. Hours later, he crossed back into the United States, into the western tip of Montana, pretty close to due north of here."

"And Susan had a stroke of lucky memory," Mike said.

"I'd pored over his prison records but missed it. When I called our office in Seattle, right after I heard that he was inside Montana, a U.S. Marshal who is moving to the FBI let it slip that a SWAT team was already on the ground here. They knew where he was. In other words, they had a tracking device on him."

"On his truck?" Annie couldn't make sense of what Susan was saying.

"No, on his body. In his mouth, to be specific. In prison he'd had some dental work. With the news that he was somewhere in Bitter Falls, Mike and I went to Albion House. The sheriff's department covered this house. We saw you arrive, and we were coming around the east end to come in the front door and warn you, but all hell broke loose before we got there."

"In the dark, with two innocent bystanders, we couldn't fire," Mike added. "We were moving to take Roth down, physically, when you flattened him with the fire foam. Great job!"

Tears gushed out of Annie's eyes as she remembered, in vivid detail, how Peter had pulled Savannah away from her.

"All right," Tess said with authority, "that's enough instant replays. Annie, you have a choice. You may either go back to bed—here, and now—or you will be back in the hospital. Your call."

"Since you put it that way," Annie said, "Goodnight, moon."

Jack walked beside her like an outrigger as she headed back to bed. Before she lay down on the double bed, he moved Savannah over.

"She's an awful bed hog," Annie whispered.

"So am I," Jack said with a chuckle. "But I hope you'll marry me before you find that out for yourself."

"What did you say?" Nothing that had happened seemed real to her. This crazy statement was simply one more mystery.

Jack knelt beside the bed and held her close in his arms.

"I'm asking you to marry me," he said. "I've been a fool, thinking I have it in my power to protect Marcy, and you, and Savannah, from all enemies, foreign and domestic. But all I have is love. All we have is each other."

He leaned forward and pressed his lips against hers, and she felt lighter than air. More powerful than a locomotive...

"I'm afraid to go to sleep," she said. "I'm afraid this isn't real."

"It's real. I promise you, it's real. I'll ask you

again in the morning, when you feel better. And I'll ask you every morning until you say yes."

She closed her eyes and drifted into a sort of twilight sleep. "In the morning," she said on a long exhalation of breath, "in the morning, I'll say yes."

Chapter Eighteen

Jack watched Tree Autrey make one last tour of the patio, checking for the tenth time on the bar supplies and the barbecue. His wait staff, in black jeans, white shirts, and red string ties, were busy in the three tents, setting the last few places for the dinner. Inside, out of the sun, a woman placed yellow roses around the four-tiered wedding cake.

"Are you sure you haven't done this before?" Jack asked.

Tree laughed. "Not for myself, but, yes. We've had weddings at the ranch before."

"If it gets any hotter, I think you should hold the wedding in the pool." Jack hooked a finger inside his collar. Today—June twenty-first, the summer solstice, also known as Midsummer's Eve—was on track to set a record for the date.

"Tree?" The minister standing at the edge of the patio looked at his watch. "You, too, Jack. Almost showtime." He motioned them to walk with him around the tents and out to the side of the seated guests.

Tree's long-time employees, Dusty and Lefty, who would be the best man and second groomsman, joined them at the designated shade tree. At the same time, and with regret, all four of the men in the wedding party put on the western sports coats they'd carried over their arms.

Single file, they followed the minister in front of the seated guests. At the bottom of the three steps, he stood aside. Then he followed them into the gazebo, where the five of them sat on benches against the curved walls to await their cue.

"Ah, at last," Jack said. "Shade." He looked the structure over with a builder's eye, wondering if the gazebo on the drawing board at Albion House should have a more open entry.

A string quartet played music from Mendelssohn's "A Midsummer Night's Dream." The guests fanned themselves. It was a good thing Tree and Tess hadn't commissioned an ice sculpture. Again Jack tried to loosen his collar.

"Hey, it's not your wedding," Dusty said with a laugh.

"I wish it was. I've wasted too much time single."

Once Jack had talked Annie into marrying him, he'd wanted to elope, but all the women in his life put the kibosh on that idea. Tess and Tree's wedding would get all their attention. Once it was over and Mr. and Mrs. Autrey were home from their week-long honeymoon in Hawaii, the Riker women, plus Marcy, would make an honest man out of Jackson T. Cabrini.

They'd made plans, of course. Women with weddings on their minds were a *force majeur.*

"Just tell me when to show up and what to wear," he'd said to Marcy with a long-suffering sigh. The honeymoon, however, was all his business. Nothing they said would wheedle it out of him. He'd told Annie to pack her passport, but that was a red herring. They were going to Marina del Rey in Los Angeles to board a twenty-eight foot sailboat and sail west to Catalina Island and south to San Diego. One glorious week with no one but each other.

Before Annie said yes, she agonized about Albion House. She'd moved to Bitter Falls fully intending to live there with her daughter and her sister. Their dad was going to get a place of his own, not far away. But her dad had decided to remarry and stay in Seattle, and Tess would be living at the Rocking Star.

It took some talk to finally convince her—kind of like it took some rock whacking to make Mt. Rushmore—that a hired manager, living in the downstairs suite, should run the day to day operations of Albion House. Tess would help with reservations and special events, and Annie could do as much, or as little, as she wished.

More than once Jack had said, "You own Albion House. It doesn't own you." It was the same litany he'd used on himself about Great Western Construction.

And yet, no matter how persuasive Tess's arguments in favor of the plan, and no matter how Jack pleaded his case, Annie was ambiguous. And then, like an answer to prayer, Vera Stefano's niece and her husband dropped by Bitter Falls to visit her.

Holly and Gabe had sold their successful restaurant in Denver, bought a large motor home, and traveled around the United States for three years, calling the adventure their temporary retirement. They needed to go back to work at something—absolutely not a restaurant, they both said with a shudder—and they wanted to live in a house again. Managing Albion House would be perfect for them. Vera was thrilled to have family so close. And the deal they'd struck was that they'd be gone, south to Arizona in their motor home, January and February.

Jack caught Holly's eye and waved. Vera, too, looked at him and gave a big smile. The music stopped, and people looked around expectantly.

"Gentlemen," the minister said. "Let's take our places."

The string quartet began playing the Wedding March, and Jack turned toward the patio. Coming out the door was Marcy. She stepped gingerly across the flagstone patio and stopped at the beginning of the white carpet. She looked from side to side, flashing a special smile at Vera, who was seated on the aisle in the second row. In the front row was Giselle Riker, looking distinctly uncomfortable. Jack knew it had taken diplomacy by Tess to get Giselle to attend.

Marcy stepped on the carpet and came forward in small, slow steps. It seemed to Jack that every third day this girl surprised him by looking older. She'd already surprised the hell out of him by being wiser.

He'd flown with her to Denver and survived the excruciatingly painful process of waiting outside the courthouse while she testified before a grand jury. Indictments had not yet been handed down, but the district attorney met with him at a coffee shop and said Marcy's testimony had put them over the top. Seeking justice was a lot like shoveling sand off a beach, he'd said, but in this case, they knew what winning looked like.

Marcy reached the steps of the gazebo, and Jack saw a look of panic cross her face. She looked at him and down at her feet. He saw at a glance that the heel of her shoe was caught in the long satin skirt.

Quickly, he moved forward, bent to free the skirt, and held out his arm to escort her to the center of the gazebo.

"You're the most beautiful girl here," he whispered.

"Thank you."

He turned and took his place in the lineup in time to see the most beautiful woman start down the carpet. Annie's ankle-length dress, like Marcy's, was lavender. At her waist she carried a small bouquet of white blossoms and a single yellow rose. He'd been told the proper name for it was a nosegay.

Thirty days and counting. He and Annie would have a small wedding in a chapel on Main Street. One with air conditioning, thank God.

She made it up the steps without mishap and stood beside Marcy. Jack followed her gaze back to the white carpet. At the far end, looking small and regal at the same time, stood Savannah. Her dress was white, with lavender and pink bows catching up the hem like bunting, and a wide pink ribbon at the waist. On her head she wore a crown of orange blossoms.

With practiced precision, she paced her way down the aisle, scattering rose petals ahead of her. At the steps, she flashed him a huge smile and took her place to Marcy's right.

The guests stood and turned to see Tess and her dad, Paul Riker, start down the carpet. A communal "Oohhhh" showed the unanimous opinion. She was beautiful, wearing a simple lace dress in Victorian style and a short veil. Jack stole a look at Tree's face. He looked as happy as a man could be.

Annie had told him that Tess and Tree were going to start a family as soon as they could. And the first words out of Marcy and Savannah's mouths when he and Annie told them they were going to be married was, "We want a baby brother or sister."

"And here I thought having Lady and Katy live together would be all you cared about," Jack had said with a laugh.

He couldn't imagine himself holding a helpless new baby. In fact, he'd never in his life held an infant. The Riker women and Marcy all assured him he'd get the hang of it.

"Everything you learned taking care of me shouldn't go to waste," Marcy said loftily. "And you have to admit, I'm turning out better than you expected."

With the three of them, plus Aunt Tess and Aunt Vera, all making plans for babies, Jack wondered if he'd ever get a chance to hold his firstborn. Maybe Tess and Tree would beat Annie and him to it and he could get in some practice as an uncle.

In the meantime, he'd hired a subcontractor to

build on to his house. The two bedrooms and one large bathroom for Marcy and Savannah, plus a new office for himself, would be framed and closed in before winter, and he could finish them out himself. The plan, dreamed up by Annie, Marcy and Savannah—and eagerly endorsed by Jack—was that Marcy's current room should be redecorated as a nursery.

"It's big enough for twins," Savannah exclaimed as he sketched the plans.

"Don't you need to take Lady out to play?" he'd asked.

He listened carefully to the minister ask the age-old questions about promising to love, honor and cherish one another. In his head he practiced his response. *I do, I do, I do.*

****

Annie carried three bulky but lightweight wrapped gifts to her Ford Escape. The back and the back seat were full of gifts and flowers, so she placed the three boxes on the front seat. She'd empty it at the rental house, and Tess and Tree could open them all when they returned from Hawaii. Tess's bedroom already looked like a warehouse.

She clicked the lock and returned to the lodge. In a room down the hall from the lobby, one set aside for the bride and her attendants, she surveyed the aftermath of all their quick changes of clothes. It looked like a sea of satin and lace.

One by one she hung the dresses. As soon as Tess and Tree left, surprising and delighting everyone by riding away from the ranch in a surrey with the fringe on top, Marcy and Savannah changed into their swimsuits.

Annie had changed into Bermuda shorts and a cotton T-shirt. She intended to join the girls at the pool, but first she had work to do. All her attempts to help clear up the dinner plates, et cetera, were waved off by Tree's employees and the caterer who'd been hired for the day.

Dusty and Lefty had carried nearly all the gifts to her car and Jack's. Her only job, it appeared, was to hang up the beautiful dresses and put all the makeup and hair brushes in a small suitcase.

She sat in an armchair, glad to get off her feet. She was in tennis shoes now, but for hours she'd been in three-inch heels. Lord, how long had it been since she wore pantyhose and high heels? Answer: not long enough.

It had been a beautiful wedding, and the reception was a party to remember. She'd forced herself to spend time with Giselle, the woman who was legally her stepmother, and actually found some areas of mutual interest. Giselle had said all the right things about how beautiful and clever Savannah was, and she'd even taken off her high heels and refereed a game of crazy backward softball with the kids.

Her dad had hugged her and said, "Thanks, honey. I feel like I'm getting my family back."

"And next month you get to do all this again," she'd said, wiping tears from her eyes before her mascara ran. "Well, not all. My wedding will be much smaller."

"Smaller audience, but equally beautiful," he said. "Would it be all right if Giselle and I came three or four days early, and all of us could have dinner together? By 'all of us' I mean our expanded family, before the rehearsal dinner."

"I'd like that. No, I'd love that."

She rose from the armchair and searched for her Seattle Mariners duffle bag. Her swimsuit was there, and her towel. Good. At a light tap on the door, she called, "Come in."

"Annie, how are you?"

She turned toward the woman's voice. "Susan, hi. I had no idea you were coming to the wedding."

U.S. Marshal Susan Hightower came in and

closed the door behind her. "Fact is, I missed the wedding. I came to see you."

"Me? What now? Please don't say you want me to testify." She held up her hands as if warding off blows. "I'll do it. But I don't want to."

When Susan stopped by her house the day after the shooting inside Albion House, she'd said it would take time to sort out all the jurisdictions and all the crimes. Her belief was that Sheldon Roth's get-out-of-jail-free card was revoked. He'd committed about six crimes since he'd gotten out of the federal penitentiary, and she was determined to prove he'd paid off someone inside the federal judiciary or the FBI, or both. The trail might even lead to the door of the head of the U.S. Marshals in Seattle.

"He should be locked up for a long, long time," Susan had said, "even without being charged with attempted kidnapping of Savannah. But if we have to use it, we will. He doesn't belong on the streets of Seattle or Paris. Or on the beach at Grand Cayman Island."

Susan lifted Savannah's dress from the rack and fingered the delicate bows. She said nothing.

"Why are you here?" Annie said. "And don't tell me you can't stay away from the horses."

Susan smiled and tugged a piano bench out into the open. She sat and motioned Annie toward the armchair.

When Annie was seated, Susan cleared her throat.

"The issue of testifying against Sheldon Roth—by any name—is moot."

"Only two reasons for what you say come to mind," Annie said slowly. "Three if you count 'They let him out again.'"

Susan shook her head.

"Reason number two? He confessed to everything and got a life sentence?"

Susan didn't move her head or speak.

Annie's breath caught in her throat. "How did it happen?" Annie asked. "Where?"

"He recovered from the neck wound and was escorted to a federal lockup facility. They said they had to hold him until they got the proper paperwork. The man hired to kill him did a half-assed job of making it look like suicide."

Annie put her hands over her face.

"Fortunately, he was still alive when they cut him down. He made a dying declaration that Judge Walter Sommers had taken more than two million dollars to let him out. We have his declaration on videotape."

Annie put her hands down. "Will it stick? Will you nail the judge?"

Susan nodded. "Oh, yes. And the two men who tried to make it look like suicide testified that Judge Sommers threatened them with longer sentences if they didn't carry it out."

"When?" Annie asked.

"Last night. Sheldon lived for about an hour, but his carotid artery was too fragile to recover. I got there with maybe five minutes to spare. He told me three things. His account number at the bank in Antigua, and his password."

"You said...three things."

Susan reached over and pressed her hand on Annie's clenched fists. "He said to tell you he was sorry."

"Thank you for coming. It would have been horrible to see it on the news." She took a breath. "Do you think, with the bank information, that you'll be able to recover money for the investors?"

"It's too soon to say. I have an appointment with a federal prosecutor tomorrow afternoon, in Seattle. I'm not giving those numbers to just any Tom, Dick or Harry. There are rats on both sides of the cell doors."

"This was a long way to come for a half hour

meeting," Annie said. "I appreciate it more than you could know."

"There's a handsome horseman I plan to see before I go back." Susan smiled. "There must be something in the water in this town."

"You're welcome anytime. We'll be glad to put you up at Albion House after the middle of September. And Jack and I would love to have you at our wedding. One month from today."

"Thanks. I can't predict that far out, but it's nice to be invited."

The two of them rose and walked down the hall and out to the front porch. Dusty rose to his feet from the glider swing and strode toward them. He was known for his smile, but Annie saw that it was a lot wider when he looked at Susan Hightower.

Susan held out her hand to shake, but Annie hugged her instead.

Without turning, she felt Jack behind her. She turned slowly and closed the distance between them, first with a kiss, then with a fierce hug.

"We have to talk," she said, "but I'm not sure where to start."

Talk, and swim, and play "backward softball" with our kids. And work hard. And get married, and make love.

"I love you," Jack said. "That's a good place to start, isn't it?"

She nodded and wiped the tears out of her eyes. "Always, yes. Always a good place to start. I love you, too." She put her arms around his waist. "Let's go for a walk by the pond."

Thank you for purchasing this Wild Rose Press publication. For other wonderful stories of romance, please visit our on-line bookstore at www.thewildrosepress.com.

For questions or more information contact us at info@thewildrosepress.com.

The Wild Rose Press
www.TheWildRosePress.com